Other books by Sherrie DeMorrow:

The Knight and Daye series:

Knight and Daye
Cloud of Dreams
The Elder Rose
All The Land
The Little Bird
Beyond the Land
A Little Princess
Romancing the West
The Silver Millions
The Painted Chapel
A Hound's Desire
Space of Things

The Young Dr Huer series

A Beginners Realm

A BEGINNERS REALM

BY

SHERRIE DEMORROW

Published 2021 by

Lightning Source (UK) Ltd
Chapter House,
Pitfield,
Kiln Farm,
Milton Keynes
MK11 3LW,
UK

Dr Huer character and Buck Rogers in the 25th Century©, tm by the Dille Family Trust, All Rights Reserved

Buck Rogers in the 25th Century TV series© Universal Studios, All Rights Reserved

Any place names or characters from the TV series were used solely as reference, with no intention of infringement of intellectual property rights of the aforementioned.

All rights reserved. No part of this publication may be reproduced, stored in a retrieval system, or transmitted, in any from or by any means, electronic, mechanical, photocopying, recording or otherwise, without the prior permission of the publishers.

© Sherrie DeMorrow 2021

Cover Art Design by Sam Wall

*In Memory of Tim
With love*

PREFACE and AUTHOR'S NOTE

Please be advised this novel is a backstory of the character of Dr Elias Huer of the *Buck Rogers in the 25th Century* series, old and new, but I am basing it on the television series that aired from 1979-81. However, the events in this story PREDATE the television series, and cover Dr Huer's younger years, up until the series itself. Then the story ends.

I did write to gain permission from Universal to use this character, but I got no answer. Hence, I am writing these new series of books in loving tribute to the man who portrayed Dr Huer in the television version, Tim O'Connor. Tim has made appearances in several of my books, re-imagining a character for him in the *Knight and Daye* series that I just completed. This story does draw from those books, to put a cohesive backstory to the Dr Huer character. I want to give the man more than just a 'desk job'. I want to see what his early years were like, for example: what he thought, how he lived. Was the 25th century all that it was cracked up to be, as it was shown on television? Why did Dr Huer seem so sad? I want to see the good doctor in action, like Buck Rogers from the previous shows. A lot of the time, the doctor was so dead-pan serious, it made me wonder. An actor of the older generation would display vast amounts of seriousness to a role that was expected to be serious. However, the portrayal was so good, it made the character dull and boring. I do not believe (and I refuse to believe) that he was really like that. There is much to explore, and to examine the nature of Dr Huer is an excellent example of fandom, indeed.

Some place names and characters given are based on the television series (like New Chicago, or Anarchia, Kane and Twiki); acknowledgements for this had been made previously. Other characters, mentioned or otherwise, are fictional and loosely based on people known of by the author, or from the previous *Knight and Daye* series. Any personalities referred to herein are used (again), in loving tribute.

If there is anything amiss, please write to the publisher, and it shall be corrected.

CHAPTER I

It was a world... a world that was sitting within a dehydrated milk bottle in the middle of a cat's litter box. A world that was called Earth, now living in the 25th century. Such was the lives that passed on or remade, since the self-contained nuclear blast. Self-contained, in that we didn't affect anything else but ourselves; we were to blame for it. Not aliens of other worlds, nor our far off neighbours, the Draconians, could have devastated the planet in the way we did. We were responsible for the shabby mess *we* made. And we had to file ourselves accordingly, within the box that was Earth.

From recollection, it happened in the late 20th century; a catastrophic amnesia withered into social consciousness. It was a blast that nothing could measure. Not even sophisticated instruments could withstand a magnitude of that extreme. Everything was gone; we rebuilt the pieces. Those of Old Chicago would remember, but from what I was told, most of the population were struggling, blithering idiots, possibly affected by the nuclear radiation, possibly affected by themselves. Records of the period were lost; so they could not prove when the occurrence happened. Those among us who could discuss it, had refused to. They wanted to get on and be nobody special. Those that wanted to *be* special, did so at their own risk. People won out, or were scattered to dust, either literally or metaphorically. *It was up to the person to decide.*

The stars retained their elements, but there was a curio that was noted by the survivors of the putrid blast, and their offspring. One star, maybe an asteroid (or a spaceship, even, according to some circles) in particular, floated around the outer planets of the solar system. It could have even travelled out further, but it was unknown whether it did or not. Upon inspection, the new phenomena was too far away, and looked too blurry in the telescope. Despite our advanced age of time and progress, some things needed improvement. That went for a few things.

We were too busy trying to rebuild Earth, founding cities, with *New* in their title, such as communities like New Chicago, or New Manhattan, New Phoenix, or New Amsterdam. At least we rebuilt our society, from whatever leftovers you can muster from the fridge. Previous generations preferred to name their city New Chicago, mostly to pair it away from what was left of Old Chicago. It was left to us to rebuild civilisation on fallow ground, even going as far as celebrations for ourselves when necessary.

And with busyness comes emotional drain. People were exhausted, people needed a welcome break. The star looked stronger in some parts of the sky, in other parts, it dimmed. When it got stronger and brighter, people took it for a sign, or something.

The primitives at Anarchia were one such folk who loved to revel in their archaic beliefs and simple *man-hunter vs. me* structure. Yet, we needed something too, to believe in. Most of us were over that dreaded nonsense, taking up with computers and advancing them to the point of running the place themselves! However, there were some who really felt they needed *something* to get them through the weariness.

So the more intelligent of us started to search, out there. Not in spaceships, mind; not yet. They wanted to clear our world from its debris, and from the sleek look of New Chicago, they did a pretty good job of it. There was not much else to do, except wait for a miracle. And it was that travelling star show, or asteroid, or ship they saw; but, where did it come from? Was it from our time, or from the halcyon days of 20th century earthbound science fiction? Better yet, was it science fact?

No one knew; those who were not of the scientific ilk had seen this star too, with the aid of a *penny-a-view* scope you can see on the shoreline.

They laughed about it and thought it would be great to hold a festival for this star, known as the Januard. just for the sake of forgetting the Blast and getting on for their futures. They appealed to all walks of the scientific community about it and the community was in agreement. They thought a day of disposal should not carry humankind *that* far from the goal of re-evolution.

Emotions went as crazy as a florist's shop. People hungered for pleasure; they had enough pain, even as descendants. No one cared. They were ready to *party*. And party they did. For a few generations, people gathered in New Chicago, by a brimming fountain in the main square. There was a bandstand, too, which was enthusiastically used by musicians who studied what was left of the old, taking in the new with stride. *It was their songs.* There was much to be excited about. A scientist, probably an ancestor of mine, looked up through his telescope and saw the star-fix. Everyone whooped about and enjoyed the mayhem, albeit calmly. We were emotional, yet contained in the constraints of society.

The festivities lasted a day, then it was back to work for the many. For the few, they still enjoyed their usual hangovers until the police set them correct. We didn't break out in a mob, become violent; oh, no. We were civilised folk and we knew it. We survived the Blast and lucky enough to do so. We thanked whatever-it-was-that-could-be and got on living and rebuilding.

There were settled communities in both, yet one lived beneath the salvaged line. Old Chicago was made up of survivors of the Big Blast, who reverted back to primitive ways and methods of life. Was it their choice? I don't know, and I'm not here to go philosophical about it. They were feared by us in New Chicago, just as the old gangs of the early 20th century; however, this was for a different reason.

We in New Chicago didn't approve of their spineless and scrappy ways; I did not care for them in the slightest, though I left much room for doubt. Such is the way of the scientist. You never knew who would be living there, and you cannot judge all by a few.

I was born Elias Huer on July 3, 2439, along with my twin brother, Silas. My father, Elias Huer, Sr, was a scientist whose footsteps I would eventually follow, and my mother was Numara Huer. We lived on Jossi Hill Road, in the area of the Mackeon Fields. It was a nice district, and quite affluent. My father was most demanded of by many, and thankfully, well-paid for it.

The early leanings of boyhood were not unfathomable, nor unmanageable. Milk bottles littered the room where Mother was racing down the track to ensure we were well-fed. There were no complications in health for either of us. When we had a sniffle, it disappeared naturally. Must have been the air in the place that'd done it. One time, there was a surging virus. I vaguely remember Father going out to work in his bio-suit, while Mother stayed with us at home. Of course the virus was eliminated within days, such was the power of our science and medicine, along with Father's help.

Communication was also jovial, our baby talk lit up a room. Having the two of us in tow, Mother must have had a real laugh. Imagine two little Huer babies about to make the greatest leap of their lives! We had much fun together.

To look at Father, you can see a tall, lean fellow in his late 50s, with blue eyes and a serious face, devoting his life to science. He was never slovenly, and always neat in just the right places. Even when he sat down to read his intellectual periodicals, his pants wouldn't crease up on him. He was a great fellow, but slightly distant. It bothered me sometimes; how I couldn't reach out to him. He just was *there;* stern, yet loving.

You never knew what he was thinking, either; he kept much of *that* to himself. He also harboured a secret, nothing in a nasty light, but worth the discussion. Since the nuclear debacle of our civilisation, an ancestor called Timothy Daye changed the family name. He figured that in his day and age, everyone was hankering for a fresh start and he wanted this for himself too.

Father had some volumes of books in the bedroom I shared with Silas, long ago left behind by Daye, which included a story of a fellow called Conna of Cobhayr, formally known as King Muffyhuer. He reigned in the Cobhayr District of Ireland, in the more primitive time of Man's existence. (We thought anything before the Blast was *primitive*.) Timothy Daye looked at the name, and thought how cool it could be if he refashioned himself after the ancient Irish King. He liked the name Muffyhuer, but something about it didn't sit right in his mind. The Muffy bit had to go; it sounded like a pet dog's breath on a lamp-post, and the King himself was donned in furs resembling canine features. *Augh!* The second part of the name, Huer, sounded far better. *That's a name I could use.* When your world bursts like a shiny balloon into millions of pieces, it'd be quite different to pick up and find a piece to explain your own.

And so, it was decided to change the family name from Daye to Huer. Everyone else had to start over, renewing their planet, renewing their lives. This was an example of how it had affected us. No one cared either; you couldn't prove yourself anyway. Records were destroyed and word-of-mouth experience tends to be forgotten. If you move away from your original home, that too gives a person a chance to begin anew. Through the sleepless nights of those early years after the Blast, I'd wondered if he'd left something behind. It was as if he grabbed something precious, a retention of a long-lost heritage; a heritage crying out for old Ireland, and not seeing it in this newfangled place, freed from the posthumous island.

Mother was different. She came from a reasonable background, nothing flashy; nothing like Father. She was as informal and playful, as Father was crusty and scientifically formal. It was a wonder they met, let alone married! Well, when you have to start over again, *begin with the best*. She was the kind of mother you wanted for comfort on a cold rainy night. She looked after Silas and me with relish, and enjoyed every moment of her time with us. She was great to be with and an excellent barrier to the coldness Father displayed at times, when he got a little *too* serious with his work.

She used to encourage us, doing simple activities. Something that resembled baseball.

'Elias, come on,' she'd say, as I tried to make a target with a ball, crawling. *I was only two then!*

I sputtered out some sound, but couldn't hit the target. I was out. Silas was up, and he hit the ball like there was no tomorrow, only yesterday.

Mother called out, 'Silas, you can do better than that!'

'I know,' he instinctively said.

She ran to him aghast. 'What did you say?'

'I know,' he repeated.

I came over to him, still crawling. 'Goo,' I muttered, as I tried to get upright, but fell down easy.

'My little bundles,' Mother gathered us up in her arms. I felt the love. So did Silas. She cradled us calmly. 'Elias, you tried to walk didn't you?'

'Aaaahhh,' I croaked, not understanding speech.

I got up again to spite the known, leftover world. And fell down again.

'I know,' repeated Silas.

'You can do it Elias,' Mother egged me on.

I tried to walk again, and I held onto my brother. He let me through and allowed progression to be made. I believed that was the time I first trod on solid ground with both feet.

'Hey, not bad little guy,' she encouraged.

I kept walking, beyond Silas's help. I just toddled on, around the corner; around the bend, too.

I returned with a less famished heart.

'God, I wish I could...,' Mother began to rave, but stopped quickly, as we were in her realm and thought it would be offensive to rave about something natural. It should have been taken as *nothing to it*. 'Oh, come here,' she kept hugging us.

My stomach turned at the goofiness of the memory, yet I had to say she cared very much for us. Silas smiled at me, but it looked odd. It was closed mouthed. He hadn't grown out his teeth yet. Neither did I. But that smirk was to lay a threshold upon me for many years to come.

CHAPTER II

I sat in my extra large cot with Silas, muttering, drooling, and fighting, as all babies do. A baby monitor was placed on a dresser in our room. Built by Father as one of his so-called 'inventions', it was called the *Hueronic Detector Machine*. I thought we were being bugged, or spied on, to say the least. I carried on wailing, as I did then, and filled the airwaves with sound to give them something to *think* about. Teasing the twin was another mimicry I had attempted for attention; that smirk Silas gave me had reason for me to lamb-bash him on numerous occasions. Yet, with all this technology, *why couldn't I just have a buckin' baby rattle instead?*

Meanwhile, Father was doing research, with no time to spare for crawling, insect-like little ones. That was a job for Mother. He got on with his assignments, and reading boring lecture-style books. His experiments were also intense, though I didn't understand them at the time. I just saw bright vials of things, that I thought you could drink.

'No, no, Elias, please do not touch that,' Father would say to me. 'When you get older, you can help me.'

I was embarrassed. We proved to be a handful. With two rambunctious boys on her hands, he felt it better. Let her do the work. *I'll do mine.* Father thought about the greater good in society, and determined to make his mark upon it. At times, though, he would interact with us. He wasn't a scientist *all* the time! He was loving, yet distant, at the destiny set before him. What was that destiny? Well, it turned out he didn't know either. So he made an educated guess, like he did with his endless experiments. It was determined that society needed him more.

During these early runs of our lives, science rather than religion was key. There was a church in New Chicago called the Inner City Central Church.

Scientists, like Father, loved to refer to it as IC3, as a joke among themselves. It sounded like those experimental phrases they like to use in formulas. The Church took all aspects of God, and conveniently thrown them together into one faith. This all powerful God controlled the Universe, and made it right. At times He made it wrong, which explained the Big Blast and the century-old cities like New Chicago. Problem was we were to blame for the Blast, not God. This didn't deter what was left of Mankind to solve away its problems for good. Pin the tail on the donkey was a good way to explain yourself. Father saw the erroneous attitude and shied away from religion as a whole, seeing Science as Man's true saviour. I followed Father into this scientific realm of data and raw fact, and left the fates to themselves.

Yet, Silas did not. Being twins had not prevented us from pursuing our own interests. When we were away from our confining cot, we crawled around to explore the room, nay the world, with Mother's supervision. Sometimes she would leave us, switching on the *Hueronic* machine to keep tabs on us young'uns. I reckoned that no matter what or when you lived, people still kept watch over you, especially fussy mothers like ours.

While Father left the dead folks behind doing science experiments, I was called in to assist, clever that I was. *I couldn't even talk straight yet!!* Silas remained in our cosy room, looking at some books. The volumes were well-bound and thick, something a mere toddler wouldn't understand, let alone read. The age didn't deter my dear brother, and he occupied himself with fascination over them on the bookshelves. For some reason, Father allotted room in *our* space for his procreating books. There never seemed enough pages in the universe to store all that information.

One of the books Silas picked up was called, *Rituals and Reckonings in Ancient Ireland*. Left behind by the One who changed our name to Huer, it was put in our room by Father, who ran out of book space on *his* shelves.

It was unknown why such a scientific man of our household would bear interest in such a book. Yet, here it was, in its old-fashioned glory. Considering our descent from Conna of Cobhayr, and the Dayes of Ireland, I guess Father had it knocking around for old-time's sake. The volume itself was not *that* valuable by a long shot, but in some markets, someone might find it historically useful. Maybe there was a primitive streak in him after all.

Silas opened the book in a childish, clumsy way, taking some care but not really meaning it, and read about all the natural beauty of the place. Spells, incantations, power-potions, and other natural sensualities were ingested into his tiny mind. Prehistoric facts or fictions of Irish wisdom and story-telling invaded the plain-jane antiseptic look of the 25th century, giving it much-needed colour and vibe. Silas grew fond of it, not really knowing what he was reading, but there was an aesthetic beauty to it, which was hard to escape from. It seemed that he liked to sink his snout into old Ireland to get reunited into his conscious self.

He read quietly, unusual for a young tot his age, rambunctious as he was. The pictorials and drawings littered the volume, along with text. The colours in the book shone brightly like a manuscript of the era. The wording was medium print, and quite solid. There was a reference to the King Muffyhuer, a name that scared Silas silly.

I didn't think anything of it, when Silas freaked out, closed the book and ran to Mother. I sat there, dumbfounded on what he discovered. I opened the book and saw the King for myself. He was handsome, just like our father. I read the inscription, and the illustration there was just a mock-up of what he *could* have looked like, if there was a camera back then. As there was no such invention in that time, I thought the likeness was rather eerie. Haunting, to say the least. What really scared *me* was the manner of his demise.

I read that part and freaked out myself. I didn't know why. I wasn't trying to copy my brother, but I read on. He didn't. I now knew the truth about this King. Swallowed up by the earth he camp-fired on, along with his Queen, Cindihan. It was a tragic story, as earlier in time, the couple grew to love one another. The King had helped with Cindihan's familial issues, when he was still boring-old Conna of Cobhayr. The important thing was he *loved* her. Silas only looked at the name and ran.

And run he did. He didn't bother with the backstory, or what their future had beholden. He just saw the name. *Our name.* It was as if he did not care. I felt bad for someone who wanted to know our past, and yet, never took time to *read about it*. He just upped himself and ignored something very special. And so what if our name reflected that of the King's? It just showed that our descent was special, but not as special as someone who was empowered over a period of time. Muffyhuer was not; he and Cindihan were on a 'honeymoon' of sorts, when the tragedy struck. No getting out of that, and no one to claim them as their own. *Yet.*

Mother was reading one of her volumes of pleasure, when he scampered in, me following the close second. He made gestures to explain himself, as his words were hardly understood as of yet except for 'I know'. Silas took Mother to our bedroom and showed her the book, where our namesake King was mentioned.

'Yep, that's your ancestor,' she said proudly. 'And what I married into. You can see where we got the Huer name from.'

So that's why Father kept this volume!

'That King,' Mother continued, 'Although grand, didn't live long enough to see any plans into action.'

Silas muttered something that sounded like 'Why?'

As if to ignore the as-yet lack of speech, Mother answered, 'If you continue here on the page,' she pointed out the section of the book in question. 'You can see this King had fallen in love with a girl called Cindihan. When they mated, the gods took them and they became the earth,' she continued

Silas gave Mother a parched look.

'It's legend, myth, and could be true. It is too long ago to start nitpicking about it. Anyway, the town they once lived in, Cobhayr I believe, was renamed Oconnalow in their honour.'

Silas started reading again, and for some strange reason, became eloquent for a toddler. 'The spell had broken and the King became a very old man in a manner of seconds. He still loved his Queen as he died, and they became the earth they walked upon.'

He stopped, and put the book down. Reflections passed faster than a flying broomstick outside a window. He was stricken by what he'd read and surprised such a thing could have happened. It was nothing compared to the Big Blast of recent times, *but still*.

'Silas, you spoke again!'

The child felt awkward. First it was 'I know', then it was... it was as though he was being 'controlled' by a powerful entity, that faded as soon as he finished the passage.

'It's fine, and there you have it, Silas,' Mother then complimented him. 'Your reading is good. You speak well. I knew you could do it.'

The young boy looked up and gave Mother a smirk, similar to the one he gave me. He tried to say 'Thank you', but muttered gibberish again. It seemed the magic, if there was any, had gone.

'Oh, back to your old baby self now are we?' Mother took the child and cradled him. 'Anyway, this King Muffyhuer gave his life to his Queen and Kingdom. He also gave us a cool name. I mean who ever heard of a snappy scientist called Daye?'

Mother was right. There was none. Later on, it turned out a baby emerged from the ashes of Muffyhuer and Cindihan. A harsh wind took shape, screaming the name 'Oh Conna!' A young girl, Daye, took the child and gave him the name Conna, as a token of remembrance. Silas then opened the book again, and saw the stories of the subsequent Daye family take shape. Then he re-read the section on Conna of Cobhayr. It was said Conna took a potion to prevent him ageing, keeping him as a fifty year old. Fifty years wasn't young, but it wasn't old either. When he died, the King's real age fought back violently, and made him a stinging ninety year old, as he entered Eternity.

There was much to think about for young Silas. He grew fascinated by the story, wondering if spells and magic could come true in *this* day and age. He had a glint in his eye that did not go unnoticed.

So Mother asked, 'You alright, Silas?'

He grunted a 'yes', and kept reading. He wanted to get as much information on this as he could. He started getting into the section about spells and whatnot. It seemed he wanted a piece of primitiveness for himself and was taken away with the ancient lore. It was obvious he was enjoying it and pleased to have found these works to begin with. It made for an interesting contrast between us.

I walked away and left him to his primitiveness. Father wanted me in the lab, now that I was slightly older, but not by much. I wanted to help him, as much as I could, even keeping him company. I wondered if this science-bit would get me closer to him. Science had its 'magic' too, but it was more founded on the logical, and if you wanted to prove it, you needed mathematics.

So, I hung around Bunsen burners, Petrie dishes and other glass/electrical lab equipment. Hardly a place for a toddler. A normal toddler. I was not considered a 'normal' toddler by Father, and he needed assistance of some kind. Mother took no interest in his scope, and Silas, well, he was reading those primitive volumes. Experiments a-lit the room, as he searched through his microscope for answers. I did help as much as I could, pass me this or that item; don't lean against that side-bench or you will disrupt the balance of matter. That sort of thing. I took it all in, and was happy to be with Father.

I tried to think like him and make sense of everything around me. *Was I becoming him? Did I really want to be like him?* I was not sure. He was fishing through a book to find components to an experiment. I hid behind a curtained mainframe, and looked down at my thumbs, adjusting my position. I wasn't sure, where I wanted to be, though; either with Father, or Silas.

'You okay, Elias?' I heard my father call out.

I went out, and looked up at him, with much effort, 'Yuh.'

'Learning to talk are you?'

A smile ravaged my pretty face. 'Yuh.'

'Well, you'll get on soon enough. I have to prepare this molecular device to reach a quadrant before I show it to my colleagues,' he said. 'The details are intriguing and mathematics do come into their own with this.'

I did not understand what he said, but I was sure everything was in hand. I wanted to ask him about that silly volume that kept Silas busy, leaving me on the sidelines of an interesting ball game. Alas, I couldn't because I had not perfected speech yet. *Damn these early stages of life. Why can't man be like an animal and be a fully fledged adult from the start?* I was embittered at my frustration. Father stopped what he was doing.

'Son, come here,' he coaxed me.

I ran and gave him a hug that meant all the world to me.

'Book,' I tried to pronounce.

'Book? What book?'

I wanted to tell him, but did not know the words fully. So I tried again.

'Book, Silas,' was an even more ambitious attempt to associate the item with my brother.

Father, I think, understood. 'Silas is reading? What is he reading?'

Now came the real hump on the camel's back.

I attempted it, and sighed. 'Muffyhuer.'

I fell down in a trance and Father picked me up.

'You mean Silas is reading that old book in your room?'

I nodded. *Ah, that was simple!*

'Okay. I got you, now. You're trying to tell me that Silas is reading the old history book, and you wanted a go at it, right? You want to read about the magic of the old days. You want to revel in it, like your brother.'

'Yuh,' I confirmed, or tried to anyway.

'Well, the old muckery-muck is good for the short term, but we've a world to rebuild,' he stated optimistically. 'And we're doing fine for the moment. Don't hurry your young years, Elias, as they'll never pass you by again. Then you will really feel left out. I'm not forcing you to go into science. You must decide what you want to do with yourself when you become big like me, though I hope you choose it when you're a lot younger than me.'

He went back to his studies, after that minor chit-chat he gave me. At least he gave me his time. That was something I'll never forget. I looked over at what he was doing and smiled again. I couldn't tell a molecular device if it shot a wall through my head. But, he was Father and it was great to be with him. I loved him for all it was worth. Mother was great too, but Father was an enigma for me and I wanted to break down the barrier to get to know him more. I hoped my meagre attempt would prove my way toward him.

I saw the busy nature of his and decided to take a walk, away from the lab. I went off to find my brother Silas. Despite my still-young age, I tried to take this walk, or crawl, as it were. I tried my utmost, but fell down again. I did not cry. It would be stupid to cry, if not hurt. Only babies did that, *and I sure was no baby by now; I got to hang out in the lab!*

I tried to walk out of the lab, then fell and crawled around again. Soon I was rescued by Mother.

'Elias, are you okay? What have I told you about crawling? You need to walk.'

I know, Mother, I tried to say, but ended up spitting out dribble instead.

'Get up on your feet. You are not an ant!'

I tried, and fell again. I went 'Yuh' to acknowledge the outcome.

'Elias,' Mother shook her head, frustrated.

Silas joined me, and helped me up. It seems he was quicker than me in this horrid toddler stage. At least he knew *how* to walk and be a brother to me. It felt good to have him around, but I wondered what else he'd be up to in later years.

'Some of us are better at these things than others,' Mother noted.

'Better at things,' Silas mimicked. 'Eliiii.'

I gave Silas a look, as he tried to sound out my name. I should not be too hard on him. Yet *Silas* was not an easy word for a toddler to say either.

So I gave it a go. I tried to think what his name would sound like, and I blurted out, 'Silage.'

Mother nearly threw her book at me. 'Elias, now apologise. How dare you call him silage? Is he a pile of garbage or your brother?'

I didn't know it was a *real* word, but it expressed what I truly wanted to say. Silas, or Silage as I now wanted to call him formally, knew too. He looked at me, more intense, like he was reading me. I did not think I was easily readable; no toddler is. Yet, what I saw in him scared me a bit. I saw potential; I saw a light that came from him, and you could not discern as to its final direction.

I didn't care. Mother mentioned the word *garbage*. It sounded like what it meant, but the word was not meant as offence to him. *Not yet, anyway.*

Mother spoke harshly to me. 'You think you can get away with it, huh, Elias?'

I shook my head 'No'. *That* at least, I could understand and express.

'Now Elias, you do not want people to make fun of you, do you? Silas may be better developed, but you will catch up. Do not let rivalry get the better of you two. You are both fine boys. You will go far, just like Silas. Maybe farther. Who knows?'

Who knows? Mother's observation reverberated in my mind for years to come.

CHAPTER III

It was not long before Mother took us to the local park regularly, between time at nursery school and being at home. The park was a fun place to play at and it engrossed our little minds exponentially. There were ducks in ponds to marvel over, and play areas for kids to romp around in. Even the adults had benches for picnics or sitting around, to get off their feet while the children yelped and played endlessly.

I had an interest in flying. Don't ask me why, it just occurred to me that it would be enjoyable. I always wanted to fly, out on missions, examining ships and modifying flight codes. It looked like fun, but I knew I'd be stricken to become the dull dumbfuck scientist, like my father was. Yet, this did not discourage me from trying. My destiny was not set at this time; I could have gone either way.

On one occasion, much later than that saccharine-styled chat we had earlier, Father had asked me, 'What is closest to your heart, at this point, Elias?'

'Flying,' I blurted out, off-centre.

'Now son,' he lectured, 'I remember what you and I discussed awhile back, about those books Silas was reading, and you wanted something. You yearned for something. I could see it in your young eyes, Elias. You're hungry, I can tell. I do not mind for you to go out there, exploring space, and feeling the *magic* of it; but you do it as a scientist, not as a flight-combat-ready-boy! We don't have time for frivolous ancient nonsense to widen our minds with. We have to focus on our world; our world in the universe with other planets, other galaxies, and other species, be they humanoid or otherwise. You must survive, otherwise who would do my work in New Chicago? The man on the moon? That crazy star, or rock flying through space? Come on.'

I didn't like the whiz-bang attitude of the elder generation. They were like the cars of the past. Driven on gas, with a mouth to match! I was different from him. I wanted to fly. Speedy jets, all over the Earth. Maybe the proverbial pep-talk Father provided could be my fuel. It can be a 'think-tank' as such, a container where I could put my fuel of thought into it. Hey, yeah, that's a good idea. Yet, with all my silly positive notions of my own future, Father was nervous about my crashing into that star or orbital asteroid, not far from our planet.

Never minding all that memory, Silas reached my intended target, the swing area. I was jealous, as he proved he could become better than me. He talked first, walked first, and now, *flying* first. This was too much for me, as I raced him to the swings.

'Catch me if you can,' he yelled out, mounting one.

'Chucks away,' I cried back, out of my reverie, running to a free swing, and climbing aboard.

Mother called out, 'Wait boys,' but it was too late. We were long out of *her* reach. We didn't listen and raced through into our trajectory and boarded our rides, respectively. Just turning four was a minor significance for us. Being in the pilot's seat was even more momentous. I wanted to ride this thing, if it were the last thing I did. I wanted to prove myself to be a pilot, but the rudimentary always struck my path to glory. I had to try anyway, and with everything I mustered, it was an obvious situation to take advantage of.

'I bet you can't make the first wave, 'fraidy cat,' I taunted Silage, which was a nickname I decided to give my twin awhile back when I attempted speech. It sounded good, and the sentiment proved prophetic.

'Bet I can, brother,' he called out to me.

And there we were, swinging our hearts away. My heart raced with every whoosh I felt under me. Gravity took its form here, as I put effort into swinging higher. Silage did too, and soon we swung in sync with one another. I slowed myself, to allow for my own path to grow. Swinging in sync scared me a bit, because it put you *too* close with your adversary. I was starting to think of him as one, despite his brotherly status to me. I found it odd in my childhood to think like this, but it wasn't something easily explained. After all, we were both loved, and well nurtured. I thought it was the book Silage found that changed him. I don't think I changed, other than natural growth.

Mother looked on, just to be certain, before she took a seat on a nearby bench where another lady was sitting. She had a darker look about her; the coat, the hair, and overall tanned shade of hue of her skin. She wasn't completely dark, just tanned. Still, she was beautiful, nonetheless. Her brown eyes presided fairly under her darker scalp.

She spoke to Mother. 'Hi, I'm Mrs Kane.'

'I'm Numara Huer. How do you do?'

'Fine. Me and the boys have been out together, and with their wildness, a park looked the fine place to spread themselves.'

'Same here. My boys are on the swings.' Mother pointed at us.

Meanwhile, I continued to tease, 'Bet you can't go higher.'

'Bet I can,' came Silage's ready answer.

Our velocities were higher, but not dangerously so. The makers of the swing sets saw to that. I certainly was not going to test those grounds, scientifically or not. I tried real hard to out-do Silage. Our relationship took an adversarial turn, despite the fact we still loved one another, sort of. He was still Silas, but a stranger was emerging as he grew. This personality would take flight in a much older day. I sensed it, as I felt trapped by it.

I played along with him none the less, and carried on my 'brotherly obligation' to him. Naturally, I didn't want the family to know there was something between us, a new phase of being. I could not tell at this point, nor did I care. I didn't want to. Right now, I just wanted to have fun.

Speech, by this point, came more easier for us, though I believe Silage was first with his forthcoming verbiage, roughly over a year and a half ago. Technically, we were still babies, but having advances in this day and age made us a little more pronounced than most. Having a fatherly scientist made this even more advantageous. With his keen interest in reading Father's book on history (as well as other books there), he became slightly self-taught. We were both taught how to speak, but reading words on a grand scale proved the old adage about reading was true. *You can speak through reading.* It helps to have a dictionary with you, even a children's version. What made it interesting was that it shut Silage up for a few hours, while he was savouring all the stories about old Ireland. Reading now became a past-time he loved dearly.

I read too. More practical things, though, like rudimentary children's science books, and informed activities involving maths with Father. Silage found them boring, and would sulk back to his love for history and magic. It did not deter Father from teaching me the where's and what's of life in his workshop. He had me to pass his skills upon, maybe taking it too... *nah, all this thinking was making my head shrink on the swing.*

Yet, I carried on thinking. More like a scientist, this time, like Father. I did enjoy the sensation of flight, and desperately wanted to go 'out there', but I could not. I was only four and stuck with a history-crazed brother. Getting support from *him* would be futile. I thought about the swing and the maths incurred when doing so. *It was the only way I could fly.* Sitting on a swing, to match a trajectory to a certain point, only to be levelled off by gravity, then pushed the other way. It was a simple, yet complex equation. I would take my findings to Father to see what he'd make of it. Maybe there was something to this maths and science lark after all.

It was apparent that Silage and I would indeed go separate ways, firstly in interest, later in earnest. For now, we battled together as brothers often do, bonded as one; thankfully not literally. I did love him, but preferred to like him. As a friend. A close friend. Someone you knew you could rely upon to have lunch with and go no further. We were together for much of the time, and everybody around us was aroused by our growth and childish skill-levels. Predictions were common, as many people thought I would follow in Father's footsteps. Silage was more of an enigma to them and they didn't think he would do likewise. He would go in a different direction; they just didn't know where, or where to.

My swinging decreased, as two newcomers trodden upon our scene. They were scruffy; dishevelled in time, but not in appearance. Both had dark reflections about them, in eyes, hair, overall look, and it made them more attractive, similar to their mother.

Silage got off the swing by now and played in a distant sandbox or a climbing frame. I looked and it was the frame. I stopped the swing to follow him, when I passed the two boys awaiting for what I thought was the swing. I stopped in front of them, so as not to be rude.

'Hi, I'm Elias,' I introduced myself.

'Nice to meet you,' one of them said. 'My name is Silver Kane, and this is my older brother, Antssarah Kane.'

'Twins?' I asked, 'I'm a twin. Silas is over there by the frames.'

I dared not call Silas by my nickname in front of strangers, *especially if they were children!* It was a personal thing that I kept to myself. If I befriended these two in time, then, well, yeah, I'll tell them.

'Nah, we're just brothers a few years apart. Might as well be centuries,' Antssarah sighed.

'Yeah,' Silver mimicked, 'Centuries.'

I was amazed at their similar attitude to mine. Thought not twins as such, brothers are brothers, and that Antssarah's correct in talking about centuries. I wondered what it was like between them. At home. I didn't wish to talk about things like that. We were too young, fresh, alive, and wanting to have more fun.

So, I ventured, 'Wanna go meet him?'

'Sure why not,' Silver agreed, 'We can play ship defenders with him.'

'We'll have equal teams,' Antssarah added. 'Just the four of us.'

It sounded like a good idea. I looked over where Mother was sitting and saw her talking to the lady I caught onto earlier. Figured it had to be the Kanes' mother. She was so pretty in the sunlight; she looked mythological to me, from what I'd read about in the history book; melodic star signs that grab your fancy, and all that.

'I like climbing,' Silver showed off. 'Look it, I could touch the sky!'

'You can touch the sky as you can touch your butt,' Antssarah teased.

'Yeah? Least I don't have a female sounding name,' Silver chirped away.

'True, but I'm not blinded by colour,' the brother shot back.

'Silver is cool, like on a can or ship, or robot. Least I don't sound like a baking product, Antsy,' he defended.

We climbed together, when Silage entered our realm from another section of the climbing area. Course, I kept my word regarding his name.

'This is Silas,' I announced.

'Hi,' the Kane brothers responded, when Silver went, 'I'm Silver, this is Antsy.'

Silage wondered, 'Antsy?'

'My name is Antssarah,' he said.

He laughed, finding the joke funny. I found the joke *past* funny. I thought about telling our new friends about that garbage word I made up for Silas. Antssarah obviously had his fair share of name-tittering as well, so he joined me in the climb. I might just tell him about it. Silage and Silver did their own thing on the bars somewhere else, in his previous quadrant.

He asked me, 'Your brother always like that?'

'You get used to it. He's my twin.'

'If I were twinned with him, it'd be destructive.'

'He comes across as spunky. His humour is just developing. Rather petty, I'd say.' I thought it was a good time for a reveal party. 'I call him Silage.'

Antssarah giggled loudly, nearly losing his balance, upsetting his little brother, who overheard and screamed, 'What are y'all laughing about? It isn't me, is it?'

'Don't worry about it,' Antssarah soothed, trying to be the older brother that he was. 'Go on playing. I'm alright.'

I understood him. Although his age was older by a few years, but his heart was settled. He was comforting, like a father, but a better brother. *I wished he could be my brother instead of Silage!* It was obvious the other two were getting on quite famously. The bonding between Silage and myself would be a bonding I'd rather forget. Well, for now, because I liked Antssarah, despite his silly name.

'You could call me Antsy, if you want,' he said.

'Okay,' I kept on climbing.

We played further, then got off the frame to play that game of ship defenders. We hid behind trees, climbed toward the stars on the climbing frame, used the swings as spaceships, and had the see-saws as combat points. It was a lot of fun, and it improved my interest in flying more. It was fun when we jostled one another in 'space'. We yelped and frolicked about, like the kids that we were. I never had so much fun, ever. With just one person to play with, it was better to have more. Then you can make more friends and play with them.

We did that for the next half-hour or so, before our respective mothers called home-time.

'Awh, we were just getting started,' Silage whined, 'Why do we have to go?'

It seemed like just making a new friend added the pain of losing contact for awhile. I felt that pain, too, with regard to Antssarah. He seemed like a rock-steady chap whom you could depend on. I was looking forward to when we could see each other again.

Mother stepped in, 'You can play with your new friends later, Silas.'

Mrs Kane had an idea to elongate our 'playtime'. 'We could have refreshment before leaving. I saw a stall over there, where they have ice cream and stuff. Your kids are more than welcome to join us.'

Not only was she beautiful, she was a genius! I wondered how she'd fare in my father's tinker-y workshop?

Mother thought about it. 'Boys, do you want anything?'

The answer was obvious. Even by *my* standards. 'Yes, please,' I cried along with Silage.

We went to the refreshment stand, where Mother bought some ice creams for us, and Mrs Kane did for hers. Further conversation and the usual mess ensued, with Mrs Kane taking most of the brunt. Those two were extremely messy with ice cream. Silage came a close second to them, and I found a drop on my shirt; Mother moaned at me. I didn't care. I had my ice cream, and I made a new friend, as Silage did. It made for a great day in the park.

CHAPTER IV

Life as a young child was exciting in the 25th century, but no different than in any other century. The exception was I had a father who was an eminent scientist of the era. In an odd fondness, the feeling was reciprocated. I grew up with a brother, however, who was more keen on the finer things of life; the budding historian, magician and all around know-it-all. Silage and I evolved together, but went upon separate paths of interest. What happened between us now fell under the bridge. *What will happen?* Well, that's another story.

Another aspect of 25th century life was the robotic entities that ruled society. There were human leaders too, but most of the thought and effort went into the pre-programmed clock-shaped boxes that twinkled like Christmas lights when you spoke to them. The models lasted as long as sentience allowed; if anything defective happened, they could be reinstated into something new, or shut down altogether.

Reinstatement was an embarrassment for the project, because the computers would think they were 'dumbed down' somewhat. This notion was anathema to them, as their higher intelligence spoke to them in song; their smugness spoke to us in volumes. They were also better equipped than humans in that regard. Sometimes people could still be stupid, despite this day and age; the computer boxes would make up for this. The lack of superior knowledge frightened many of us, who were trying to rebuild the world, as we *thought* we knew it. What we got was an advanced society, which was good, but computers ran the place. And they ran it with their own wills, a technological efficiency no man could master.

Emotions were also beyond their comprehension. They were created to do a job, not to be a playmate of sorts. They weren't there to play nursemaid to anybody. They were factual, punctual, and to a child, tedious to a fault. Yet, I was fascinated by these 'creatures' of science, and wondered what it would be like to have one of my very own.

Not to outdo my friendship with Antssarah, mind you. I liked him and his brother, Silver. There were others at school which I befriended, but the technology stood before me, prevailing a test of my time. I then thought it would be cool to have a computer friend. So one day, I asked my father once if I could have a 'boxed' companion of my own.

'You should make real friends, Elias. Go forth and enjoy your childhood like the others,' was the conceptual answer I'd get from him.

'I do have real friends,' I argued back.

'Well, Elias, go play with them and leave me to my work.'

I sighed and left the room. I hoped and prayed for one anyway. *Who knew what would come of it?*

The educational system had a few shaves knocked off or so, but seemed to prove themselves as an institution that kept us kids in line. The rebuilding of Earth was a major priority for the few centuries since the Big Blast, and the schools knew this. It didn't stop the educators from starting from scratch, and building up to something achievable. There were those who played the system, but were weeded out, as we needed people to know about the necessities of life. Rebuilding and survival, intermingled with the usual topics of history, maths, science, and cultural studies. Anything that would get Earth to reshape its destiny was key to the success of these young minds. It was *us* who were the future, and we learned to make it plausible for all to survive.

Those who couldn't care less about making the Earth work, ended up living dead end lives, in dead end jobs, like street sweeping, or janitorial duties. They were of a lesser sort, but still did contribute to the welfare of our new society, even if by meagre ways.

Yet, layabouts were still layabouts, even in the 2440s! A later date does not give you a better timepiece. It just gives opportunity for people to achieve for themselves; for the Earth, too, especially in the rebuilding projects. Medicine, legal and factory jobs were still desirable, just as jobs in the entertainment industry. People needed something to do when they were *off* duty, and a wide variety of pleasures were available.

Some of these pleasures were archaic in nature, like the video games of centuries past, for instance. Olden-time television programs gave a glimpse of history, and how people functioned. *Usually*, in my opinion *not very well.* Music was fun to delve into. Melodies were created against a backdrop of sunbeams, and moonbeams, with recitals at night. We had the best of culture, and it brought out the best in all Mankind.

Silage, myself and the Kanes went to school together too, but not in the same classes. We were of different age groups anyway, and I cared not to sit next to Silage in class, so as to infiltrate more with other children. There were many children to choose from, why would I wish to sit with my *brother*? During this period I found it difficult to engage with others. It wasn't because I was at fault, per se, as Silage had many friends, mostly 'at-the-time' companions. Mingling was imperative, as I wanted to break the *Huer* hold on me. Even though other companionship I still found shallow, it was a better alternative than being with *him*.

I was studious at a young age, and found it fun to learn about things, taking after my father with his seriousness in experimentation. I enjoyed the science classes with one Dr Goodfellow. He came across as a dapper man, with a smile and a handshake a-plenty. His experimentation helped us during earlier times, when he was younger. Dr Goodfellow brought things to life, helping out society with his brilliant mind. *He was a person who knew a thing or two about science.*

Much of our society was indebted to his contribution, especially with artificial intelligence. Those flickering bright lights led the masses out of their complacency and into something more unique. Goodfellow thought it would good for the computer world and our world, if we could tolerate one another. Talking to a box of lights was rather silly, but in the times when technology takes over, Man must adapt, even if it looked ridiculous. It was something to aspire to, nonetheless.

Silage was committed too, just. He, at times, would wander 'round his head a bit when the teacher got too 'boring' for him. Everything around him became boring. He was bored with lectures, he was bored with the work, and bored overall. He enjoyed being out with the Kanes, as well as other school cohorts. Playtime for him became incessant, as sometimes he would come in late. Demerits piled up, and our parents weren't too pleased. Still, he showed mental wealth in other departments, such as history, literature, and other entertainments.

Entertainments. That was all Silage wanted. He began to see the world as a more fun place to be, to take over where the builders left off and take pleasure in the world. He'd have amusement with it, and with that, he was entertained. Silage was more keen on pleasure, than in the pain of restoring our world. It did not mean we lived in the past, which would have pleased Silage a lot, but we needed a decent place to live, and the world was all we had.

Still, there was much to think about with Silage. His attitude was course. 'I read about that in Dad's book,' he'd say to me, the know-it-all that he was.

'Oh yeah,' I'd say back to him.

'Yeah, and I know we're descended from it all. Our name is from them,' he'd respond back.

I shot back at him. 'From who?'

'From those people you and I read about when we were infants.'

'You didn't take that *seriously*, did you Silage?'

There was a pause in the argument, then he made a face at me. Well, if Silage knew better, who was to debate with him. I didn't. I couldn't. I was not *trying* to be better than him, but he took it like a game of catch. Or baseball. He played like it was football though, and he'd tackle you to the ground with antiquated ideas and information, to sputter out new facts, finding new words from them. He was amazing in this manner.

His learning was acute, especially in cultural and historical matters. He still read that Irish book in our bedroom, branching out into light and magic. Library books on old folk myths and superstitions of other ancient peoples fell under his jurisdiction, too. He loved learning about them and their objects of fancy. I found it slightly creepy, and kept to myself reading my childish scientific lot. It would get more interesting when Silage took interest in other re-emerging cultures as well. Races that recovered from the Blast. People who, like us, had to start over with *their* version of society; trying to remember what was what, trying to derive what was left in their writings. A scrap of *something,* that would make them whole again.

The children in our class were alright and I liked them. They came from all sorts of backgrounds, creeds, colours, and mixes of all kinds that survived the Blast. That was okay. I wanted to get to know them, other than having a friendship with Antssarah Kane. At least with him, I proved I could have a friend. It would be great to learn from them as well, which was equally as important as learning from the classroom.

Yet, I learned passively. I liked to hang around during recess, and see what others were up to. It didn't commit me to any one person, but many. I played the field, as it were. Being brought up correctly, I was polite, pleasant, though distant, and quite similar to Father. I saw myself as an emerging character, and with those trusted qualities, I came into my own. Being cautious proved advantageous, as kids would be kids, and mischief was ever thought upon in the mind. I never got into many scrapes, nor did I wish to. I was not *perfect*, but I tried not to be too belligerent in tone.

Silage had more fun. It would be like he was an older student, going to dances, sleepovers, stake-outs, whatever. He thought his freedom was everlasting. And he shared it through his friendship with the Kane brothers. It proved fruitful, especially with Silver. I stuck with Antsy; being slightly older gave him a more meaningful time with me. He was fun to play with, when there was no one else around. Antsy was more of a wary type too, being older, yet, with me, he felt like a keen brother, not a peer.

We went together to the local cinema, where they showed old movies thankfully recovered from the Big Blast. We'd go out, with pocket money, and see these crazy flicks on the usual Saturday or Sunday afternoons. Weekday afternoons depended if school was on or not. We would go to one another's homes and enjoy the time before dinner. Sometimes, we would go to the park of origin, where we first met on the swings, to hang out. Then we'd have to go back, or they would, to eat and do anything else, then go to bed.

However, there would be one good friend that I had, that would hold the test of time.

CHAPTER V

It was our 10th birthday. Our presents were suited to our individual tastes, though. Some presents were shared, but it depended on what it was. If it were clothing, we could share it; we were relatively the same size. If it was a book, or record, or a sports-related gift, like a catcher's mitt, well, it was each to their own.

Mother helped prepare for our little party, which we invited some of our friends over. The Kane brothers came, as well as Silage's school friends. The only real friend I had was Antsy, and it was good to know him in the ensuing years since our first meeting at the park. He was not a world away, like Silage, and not going off on insignificant historical tangents. So, our friendship carried on. Silage made a great friend of Silver, and kept it going too. Together, they also incorporated other children into our small get-together.

It was nice, with cakes, and treats of finger-food, furbished by Mother. She was a wonder in the kitchen, and a damn good cook. She knew her way around 25th century versions of appliances like stoves, refrigerators, cutting boards, and utensils. After all, eating was still en vogue in our day. It seemed futuristic, yet downright homely.

Later that evening, once all the hubbub was finished and the others went home, Father came to me, with a grin on his face and intention at heart.

'Elias,' he said, 'You and Silas have been wonderful boys, growing up nicely. I have something for you both to share that I've been working on for awhile, down at the lab. It will make you alight with energy.'

Silage was sitting opposite us in a chair, reading. He perked up with, 'What will you alight us with?'

'Ah, that is to be seen,' Father exclaimed, as he called in the prize.

I groaned inside, because I thought the present was for *me*.

Father called toward the doorway. 'Come out Twiki.'

A small ambuquad came into the room, uttering an odd noise that resembled 'beading'. I thought this was normal, so I accepted it as such. I hadn't known robots were into 'beading' but, to each his own. I figured beading was an antiquated past time anyway, so I thought the sound was a tribute to the past.

Silage's eyes widened in horror. 'What the buck is that?'

Father dismissed the comment. 'This is Twiki, a drone. A toy, if you will, but he could be much smarter. He's programmable.'

I noticed two hooks at the front. 'What's that?'

He continued, 'Those hooks, Elias, are for circular circuitry. The ones who help run our society.'

I freaked out. 'You mean those computers running New Chicago? You could put a politician on here!'

'I could, if I may, but not for you. And definitely not a politician for small children like yourselves. I had not built him yet,' was his answer.

Silage droned, 'Then what is the point of this thing?'

'Well, my boy, it is a companion. A talking calculator, when the time comes. A helper. That sort of thing,' Father explained.

'Oh, like a slave,' Silage assumed.

Mother's eyes rolled; Father was dismayed. 'No, son, not a slave,' he answered. 'We never enslave any being.'

More questions of thought arose from my brother's uncompromising mouth, 'Then what are they for anyway? You can't be friends with a robot!'

'Oh but you can,' Father said. 'This one is very child-friendly, and when I get his clock-shaped companion on board, then he'll be one desirable entity.'

'You mean one desirable mess,' Silage sighed.

Mother was furious with her son. She thought gratefulness would be at his heart, for all the hours Father worked on this project. She wanted to smack him badly, to put some domination over him, to show who's boss around here.

However, in a forgiving way, Father never-minded his son's attitude of his creation, and ignored him for awhile. He sensed Silage's waywardness and accepted that this one would choose a different path. Not necessarily a better one, but a path nevertheless.

He turned to me instead. 'What do you think, Elias? Do you like Twiki?'

My mind was piqued with curious intent, and I went to the drone. 'Hi, I'm Elias.'

After some beading noises, he vocalised, 'Nice to meet you.'

Wow, I mouthed. The ambuquad certainly put a smile on *my* face, and I thought it was very thoughtful of Father to create such a character.

'You're a genius,' Mother said to Father. 'Not only that, you made Elias happy.'

He grinned, 'I know. Impressive, isn't he? It took me some time to work on him. Sorry for the missed appointments and such.'

He blushed and Mother gave him a hug. 'It's okay, Elias.'

They kept their embrace, as I looked the drone over. 'I'd say,' I was stunned. I was overwhelmed with possibilities with this fellow. Pleasantly surprised, too. 'This is neat. I'll be the envy of all the kids at school.'

'Well, I wouldn't throw around your treasures to your friends at school.' Father's concern was great. 'This drone took up much of my time, you know. Kids don't know respect.'

'They should learn,' Mother muttered, sitting down and getting back to her tablet-reading.

I walked over to the drone and gave him a pat on the head. I went across the room, indicating to him to come to me. The quad walked over, beading again, and fell into my arms. He was heavy for a small fellow.

I gave Twiki a hug, and shouted informally, 'Thanks, Dad.'

'My pleasure,' he replied. 'I've put my mind so much to science, I feel I've neglected my fatherly duties. This is to repay you.'

I kept my embrace with Twiki. 'Could he talk more?'

'If you train him, yes. There are already some things he can say now, but he can be programmed for further speech.'

Twiki kept beading again. His body was child-like, but still heavy. His face was not unusual, with eyes, nose and circuit-covered mouth in the right places. Silage ignored him, still reading. He didn't even try to say hello to him. *That would be inorganic*, he'd say.

So, I reckoned this Twiki fellow was mine. I held the drone, when Silage turned away from his book and looked at Twiki. He noticed something unusual about the head.

'Why does his head look like a.....,'

'Stop it Silas,' Mother frowned, knowing what he was on about. 'Accept what your father had given you. He's been working on the drone for several years now. And what do you have to show for it? Elias thanked him, why can't you?'

Silage turned and ranted, 'Because I'm sick of science, and its cold composure of facts, figures and 25th century weirdness. I want to study primitive matters, thoughts, feelings, people, history. Why we got here in the first place?'

'You can't blame generations of long ago, Silas, and you cannot change what's happened,' Father lamented. 'Don't take it out on us. I made the drone for your benefit, as well as Elias's. It may benefit Mankind in general, if used properly. It might even solve that mystery of the orbiting asteroid out there.'

Silage had enough of it and walked out in a huff, pouting. He reposed back in our room, getting into more sophisticated volumes about magic.

'That Silas,' Mother spoke, concerned, 'He's been cranky as of late. I thought the party with friends would set him right.'

'He's not even a teen, and already shows for it,' Father sighed.

'Maybe his development is swifter,' I suggested. 'He does have a budding intelligence, it's just mislaid, that's all.'

My folks looked at me, shocked that I would say such a thing about my twin brother, even though I gave him a compliment. Yet, never minding the attitude he displayed, I was still admiring Twiki, smiling and laughing.

'At least Elias loves your creation,' Mother commented.

'Yeah,' Father got informal too. 'It was worth it, even if just one of my children enjoys the gift.'

And what a gift it was. The drop of his senses was a surprise, but it didn't last long. Spouts of informality creep in when you are happy, and you don't even think about it. I certainly didn't. Twiki didn't either, as we played and beaded our way into the night. His sensors lit up in his personality, and he proved to be a pleasant companion for me. It was sad that Silage didn't enjoy him. It was apparent he was to take another course in life.

CHAPTER VI

As I got a little older, I found myself as a teenager with angst. Silage came into his own, too, but with a suave, sophisticated approach. He took getting older in his stride. He puffed out, preened himself, while I just did what I normally do to look good. I kept it simple. I did not want to look like a peacock like Silage. Peacocks were pretty animals a long time ago fossils of them being found around where the continent of Europe was Maybe from these fossils, they could get DNA strands and recreate these beautiful birds. Then again, if a human were to be a 'peacock', he would surely look absurd. I was likely to be the plain one of the pair. *Let Silage have himself a ball, with all the handsome feathers around him. Then we shall see who has the last laugh.*

Between us, we looked a right handful, even more so than when we were children. I felt sorry for Mother, who continually doted on us, to Dad's discontent. She would give in to Silage's wants and needs, when he should be doing things for himself. I just learned to get on and do it. Dad was proud of me, and happy to share science with me in his lab. I admired his skill, and wanted to be like him, but he unfortunately, like all good scientists, tended to be boring. Sometimes I wish he would be more of a sparkly nature, like I was as a youth. Being young had the addition of a bubbly nature, and it made life more interesting. As Dad was getting on in years, the sparkle had left him. But his eyes still shown it. He was nice to look at, at least, because of the caring and excitement he had. Yet, for all the joy he brought to me and inventiveness he brought to the world, he was *still* a boring fellow.

At least Dad had the final say in our development. 'They're men,' he'd argue with Mother. 'Let them grow in their own time.'

'I know, Elias, I know. It is difficult to let go when there are geniuses around. You just want to cuddle them some more, to get back the simpler excitements of life.'

Dad shrugged it off, and went back to his work. *In their own time.* Dad's words rang in my ear. I started calling him Dad in recent years. I didn't know why. I just did. Silage did, too, out of mockery of me. We were still at it, choking one another over our own splitting-way interests. I enjoyed helping Dad with endless experimentation in the lab, my new drone Twiki joining us. Silage had his reading kick, and grew more powerful with it. At least in knowledge. I doubted any of that old stuff would amount to anything. School was school, and everything for me was a teenage discontent. I still had an interest in piloting to explore space; Silage wanted just the world and everything in it.

'All the answers lie in those books I've been reading,' he said to me.

Sardonically, I asked, 'Do they talk about girls?'

'What?'

I repeated with a slight difference. 'Are they mentioned in the precious volumes of yore?'

Silage remained silent, though I could tell he wanted to punch me out.

'Watch it,' he warned me. 'You do not know what powers these precious volumes hold.'

'Oh, yeah,' I challenged him, 'what powers would that be?'

'How about the power to remove a sibling from the disgruntled hoard?'

I was taken aback by that comment, and questioned him no further. I thought it best to leave Silage to his 'spells' and prayed he didn't blast them toward me!

And so began our 'separation', as it were. New patterns within us emerged with the ongoing tides of youth. Sometimes they would stay, other times they went, just like the tide. Foibles became evident, and the once stable unit that was us, grew apart. Twiki didn't have much to say about 'our time of life', and took it as normal. I reckoned he was like a one-size fits all sort of gimmick, and he will move with the times. Anyway, he was good for a laugh that made you forget the squabbles of the day.

Computers were becoming more sophisticated as the years passed. It was scary to think, but some of the older models became sentient, as they programmed the new ones, with the help of human scientists, like Dad. It felt odd to me that a clock-shaped machine could change and evolve over time, by themselves, mind you. It was even more questionable that the respective unit could evoke a memory, or a dream, imagining yourself in its place. Then the unit would describe the enrichment of touchy-feely circumstances, like a kiss, a sunrise, or a shouting match between opposing sides. Colours, smells and touch were covered as one in their mind. The computers got even further, to 'turn you on', with a mild passion of a whim. Not something to think about when you think of these machines as nothing more than a box of Christmas lights on a council-induced meeting. They would be a boon to watch! *It would be a wonder to see if anything would be accomplished at those meetings.*

Twiki wasn't like that. His attitude was a cog-in-wheel type. He knew he was part of a larger system, almost a society, at that. A mechanical sprout of sorts that you programmed slowly. *It was no wonder we blasted ourselves out of the skies.* Now to begin afresh, ambuquads like Twiki were the first steps toward rebuilding society. Ours and everyone else's. They were companions, very good ones too, but some had a smart mouth on them. It all depended on the mind behind the little creatures of technology. People sometimes like to effect their own personalities into these quads, and it would show in their actions.

People thought it would be amusing to get them to say silly things and use them upon one another. Like when you were little and you looked up all the naughty words in a dictionary. Somehow, being in the 25th century hadn't changed all that. People were still people and their minds were as dirty as ever. Yet, we never broadcast this widely. It was more a little kid thing more than anything else. I feared my ancestor who changed the family name to Huer had a hand in this mechanical revolution. Maybe he did, I was unsure. I didn't care. I loved Twiki as he was, and I programmed him according to *my* style of thought. Twiki was still my friend, and ever under control. I did teach him things, but not the naughties. I learned about his programming with Dad's help, as I went along. As I enjoyed being with Dad and Twiki, I knew I was helping society, in creating these little personable figures.

Silver and Antsy Kane were in school with me and we remained friends, despite us being in different classes from one another. We were of varied age groups, but for me and Silage. They were a constant feature in our house, as we were to theirs. Silver would go off to play with Silage, and I won the day with Antsy. We usually talked about stuff, you know, boy stuff. Sometimes our respective brothers would join in the conversation, and other times, it would be Silage showing off his magical knowledge. He loved demonstrating trickery and telling tales of the legends he'd read about, especially those regarding Cindihan and Muffyhuer.

'That's where our name comes from,' he'd proudly say.

Silver went wide-eyed. 'Gosh, your history goes back nearly two and a half millennium.'

'I'd rather them call you lot Muffy,' Antssarah joked, 'It suits you. People can run after you and give you a big hug.'

He laughed hysterically, and Silage wanted a piece of him.

Antsy then backed down. 'Well, we're just Kane. Nothing special about us. We make ourselves special; nothing wrong in that. Still, think it'd be cool if...'

'Watch it,' Silage cautioned.

For a change, Silver and I were on the same side, and we laughed like crazy over it.

'Bet you two could be special,' Silage sneered at us.

We stopped laughing enough for Silver to say, 'How? Reading those history books of yours?'

'Maybe,' Silage spoke undeterred, 'I've learned a lot from them books.'

He went on to talk about the ageing spell put upon Muffyhuer, during his courtship with Cindihan, when he was still Conna of Cobhayr. It was imperative that he did this, due to the vast age difference of the two historical figures. Later, Silage treated us to simple magic tricks.

'Watch,' Silage announced, getting a deck of cards, 'Pick a card, and keep it to yourself. I will guess which card you have.'

The cards were shuffled scrutinously by Silage. We all took a card, and I found I ended up with a joker! The Kanes looked at their cards, and hid the details to themselves, respectively.

'Silver,' Silage began, 'You have a three of clubs.'

'Diamonds, actually, but the amount is correct. Three of diamonds.' Silver put his card down to show.

'Okay, Antsy, you've got a queen of hearts,' Silage called out.

Antsy giggled at the stab and revealed his card to be the ace of spades.

He sighed. 'Alright, Antsy. And you, brother Elias, have the joker, cos that's what you are!'

How did he know?

I revealed the card and, as he thought, it was a joker.

Silage shouted in victory, 'YES!'

It was at *my* expense, though. I wasn't very amused by this card game, and thankfully, to break *his* spell, Twiki came in at this point to say hello to us.

'Hi, Twiki,' Silver waved.

The drone answered, 'How ya doing kids?'

'Fine,' Antsy responded. 'This is some machine, Elias. You are very lucky to have him.'

Twiki answered, 'You call me a machine. Ho boy!'

'That's 'oh boy,' you dimwit,' Silage corrected.

'It's okay,' I consoled Twiki, giving him a hug, 'Don't worry about Silage.' I turned to the Kanes, 'Dad made him for me.'

'For us, dear brother,' Silage slurred, 'Don't forget now.'

I have had it with the attitude he gave me and shouted back, 'You didn't want him. All you care about is your dang books and magic tricks!'

'Science is cold. History and passion are the thing, really,' he snapped back.

'Only in how you *treat* science; it can be very interesting,' I defended thinking about Dad in his lab. 'It's Dad's genius that built Twiki in the first place. For us.'

Knowing a heated argument was brewing, Silver and Antsy looked at one another, then asked Silage, 'Can you show us another magic trick?'

Silage agreed, as it was uncouth to fight with friends over, and demonstrated some more magic, poorly I might add, in my opinion. We mulled over it for awhile; then it was time for us to have dinner and the Kanes went home afterwards. It was nice to spend time with them, but the camaraderie between them and Silage was astounding.

CHAPTER VII

Another step of growth continued in my path, as I was now eighteen, a young man, along with Silage. We were a two for one deal, as all twins were. It wasn't much of a deal for Mother, as she kept up her doting routines upon us until the end. Her love for us was great, and nothing would discourage her from wanting to show it, even in these advanced times. Silage felt indifferent about it, but knew she cared about him. I loved the tenderness she shared with me, though it was hard in the beginning. Her earlier harshness to me became soft, pliable and forgiving.

One day, she went out to do gardening work, then suddenly developed a fever. It made her faint, and I rushed out to get her. I asked Silage to help me, which he did to his credit. We placed her on the sofa and got her some water to ease the problem.

'That's much better, guys. Thank you both,' she said to us.

We didn't know if it were the flowers she was planting or the atmospheric conditions that tainted her system. I knew flowers had pollen in them, but getting an aliment from them was news to me. It was not a bad day, either. The weather was reasonable; a low sun with moderate temperatures. It would be pleasant to be outside that day, but then, who knows what could be in the atmosphere?

Silage and I spent days in vigil for Mother, making sure she was okay. We took turns cooking the meals, doing house chores, in addition to attending school. It was a tense time for us, and pretty sad, seeing Mother there, just languishing about on the sofa.

The fever never passed and she died from it shortly thereafter. It was sad for me, as she laid there, wilted and torn, like a balloon that just popped. There was nothing the rest of us could do, and thankfully, it wasn't contagious. None of us got ill from being around her.

Yet, it turned out to be a freak of nature that even scientists couldn't avoid in the 25th century, no matter how much technology and comfort there was. People were still people; flesh was still flesh, and we all succumb to something. It was a fact of life then as now. There are better cures and livelihoods these days, but there was the *odd* bug that went around, which took people by storm, no matter how healthy they were.

Her funeral was immediate, due to infection control, though other people had the bug too, with varying degrees. I found it terrible, and I tried not to shed tears. A boy of eighteen shouldn't cry, but this time, I had to. Silage didn't and tried to show for it. He succumbed, anyway, and I was correct in my earlier statement. It was just *how* we succumb. We both now had to display ourselves well, as best as we could, and help Dad in whatever he needs. Now, he was needy, and it was up to Silage and me to fill in for Mother, like we did when she was sick, only on a more permanent basis.

With us three men in the family, Dad had to be more proactive in helping us into maturity. Just because we were eighteen didn't make us mature in the slightest. Everyone matured at different rates, and we were no exception. Though Dad didn't have many friends, he did have many acquaintances around to ask for help if he needed it. We pitched in with our share of home duties, and one of Dad's colleagues from the lab came by to cook. It was nice to have company around the house, even if it were scientific company.

After school and during weekends, Silage and I went around to the Kanes, double dating, double dealing, and enjoying our latter teen years. Silage was getting better with his magic tricks, as his knowledge became more intense. Sometimes, it frightened me when he displayed amazements and wonder. It was weirder when he was at it with a tarot deck, and reading the cards which revealed good and bad fortunes. *It was all a luck with the draw*, as they say.

Silage was really getting off the track, but he made a decision that would separate me from his squander.

He said one day, 'I'd like to go to college elsewhere.'

Dad looked up from his test tube array. 'What? You haven't even begun to grow!'

'Well, how would I know, if I don't test myself out in the real world? I am not your experiment, you know.'

That got him. Using science for a free-for-all. 'Well, are you old enough to know your core values, morality, and survival? You feel you're ready?'

'Yes,' Silage assured him. 'Maybe to another planet, say Dracos? The Kanes are planning to go, so I'll have friends already.'

'That will extend your Earth-bound tendencies, for sure,' Dad muttered.

I smirked in the background, knowing what *tendencies* Silage was after.

Dad noticed. 'And what are you laughing about Elias? I had not seen you driven toward a goal.'

'Well, I still want to pursue flying, but you'd kept me in your lab all these years. Piloting the stars would be a great experience for me.'

'That was when you were a child. Flying is a childish past time. I was sure you'd given that up a long time ago.'

I hadn't. I still wanted to be a pilot, maybe even an explorer, searching for that Januard star, asteroid, or ship. That way, I will know about it *first*.

'Please, Dad,' I begged.

Now it was Silage's turn to laugh. 'Maybe there's a better fate for my brother, here. Going off to explore the heavens. Well, it's the heavens that determine fate, dear brother!'

I glanced at him quickly. I didn't like the sound of *that*.

Dad carefully thought about it for a few minutes, then proposed his own venture upon me, one which really blew my mind. 'You want to explore, my son? Go out to Anarchia. You can explore the farthest reaches of the city without getting singed.'

'The outer city,' I gasped.

'Yes, the ruins of *Old* Chicago. Go live with the mutant freak people and be a man. Before she died, your mother was thinking of you not to be a soft-spot within an administrative heap, like me.'

This was not like Dad, and personally uncalled for. I continued to cry out, 'What?'

'I argued with her against putting you in a boring Directorate desk-job. Naturally, I took the opposing view. I think you'd look nice behind a desk. I did, once upon a time, and you will fill the seat well.'

Fill the seat well; was I hearing this correctly?

Silage laughed continuously, and it came out as a roar. 'Elias a desk jockey. Oh, this is too much. Explore the outer reaches of a filing cabinet! He will probably come across an artefact that hadn't been seen in years; a rotten apple.'

He ran out of the room, still laughing probably to call Silver and fill him in on the action now taking place in the lab.

I stuttered, 'But, but...'

'No buts,' Dad ordered, 'You are to go out and fend for yourself. Be a man. Silas wants to attend school on Dracos. Now, that's a manly place. What are you planning to do?'

I didn't know at the time, but Anarchia was not part of it.

The last thing I heard Dad say was, 'Go out and be a man, Elias.'

So this was what I'd set out to do.

* * * * *

It turned out Dad was correct in sending only one of us to school. Mother's insurance policy and payments only went so far. We were both to go away, yet Silage was the one to benefit most. He would want the whole hog of a planet to get further education, and more freedom with his books. It would be a certain testing ground for him.

Silage picked it like the ripest fruit on the tree. I seethed inside, knowing it hadn't been me. *And I was the one to go into desk service????* It greatly upset me how it looked as if Dad favoured Silage's education over mine. Still, considering the fact Silage loved history, artefacts, and primitive whatnot, my destiny would have suited *him*! Thinking about what culture would emerge from the long-plain deserts of Anarchia; it was unfathomable. I could not even imagine people of any kind living over there.

Silage would have a field day, learning about a new, emerging-from-the-wreckage culture, meeting current folk who live rough and feeling their pain and triumph. Personally, I think it is an opportunity wasted on the wrong person. If I was to go into administration, why would Dad send me to the most unconstructive place in Man's recent history? I reckoned his decision for my going to Anarchia, or Old Chicago, would be a testing ground for me. I didn't know what was out there, or even how to get there. *There wouldn't be signposts to a dead city, would there?*

I left home unceremoniously, saying my final goodbyes to Silage and Dad. For Mother, a quick prayer would suffice, but it would take more than a prayer to get me through this thing. I didn't know if I would ever see them again, or what or who I would bring home on my return, IF I returned. The real question was if I was man enough to undergo such a feat. I was young, I admitted, but you could only go so far with being young. Things try you and age creeps up stingingly fast, like that Irish King that Silage read about. I did not think it would be like *that*, but the feeling would not be attractive.

So, I walked along the streets of New Chicago, with its people buzzing in ambiance, clinical living spaces staying pure and clean, and streets you could eat your dinner off of, without crockery. I made my way toward the outer areas, where I rested, and went to a hotel to spend the night. I missed my home already, and was unhappy with having to sleep in strange beds, with strange silver-lined linens. The night, though, proved uneventful, with ordinances preventing certain dalliances. *That* was normal in the 25th century.

I then decided to make my way out in the morning.

CHAPTER VIII

I felt I was travelling for miles, such as a vagabond would in the past. I am sure they still exist in our time, but I cared not to look for them. It was a curiosity as to why Silage didn't go on this trip with me, instead having to opt into schooling on the distant planet of Dracos. Somehow, I thought in his older years, Dad favoured him over me, giving *him* a cushy education, while putting me to the 'test' in Anarchia. Furthermore, I believed he saw me as a spoiled, but brilliant scientist like himself, but I wasn't certain. Another Elias Huer in the world would never be enough to fight against the chaos of life. *I wanted to do better.*

I left behind little Twiki too and that greatly upset me. I could have used his knowledge out here. But, my dad needed him at his laboratory. *'A drone, a drone, my laboratory for a drone,'* he'd paraphrase. I could not see myself with Twiki, scurrying along deserted paths that were once glittered with life and livelihood. He might rust in such tumultuous weather, as well, and the dry air would not be conducive to a drone. Besides, if I do meet with someone, Twiki would become like baggage for me to worry about. Nah, I think Twiki was better off being in New Chicago. Maybe his sophistication would increase by the time I return. Still, I missed his style and funny humour. It annoyed me to be so alone, but here I was, so alone.

The plains ahead of me laid bare. Desolate and Spartan, if anything. I made my way through the rocky mounds, and baked under the intense heat of summer, or of nuclear fallout, if there still remained some. In any case, it was harmless by now, and still desolate. It wasn't what I'd planned to do, once I completed my formal education. I didn't expect Silage to lay idle either. But I did not expect the favour he got from Dad, going off to another planet and such. It made me jealous; he was all set to travel to another life, as I was to embark on a new one myself, but a more scruffier existence. The Kanes went with him, oddly enough. I guess there must have been many spots to grab from at that Draconian college of his.

I walked and climbed my way through the rubble. It would have made a builder's dream come true, if not for what was glowing beneath. The glow was not intense, just there. I didn't think it was harmful by now, centuries after the Blast. I could not help but see how bare and pale everything was, compared to the squeaky clean sheen of New Chicago. *It was certainly an adventure, all right.*

I thought about someone who would want to lay a foundation out here, and came up with, 'I think I'd build another planet here,' the builder would say, whimsically.

The mind changed quickly, focus bearing down on my very being. It was hard to be alone in this acrid wilderness. I can see why they created New Chicago out of all this mess. I walked and walked. Minutes turned to hours. My throat was parched, and there was not enough water in my canteen to sustain me. *I thought I'd pass out, and I nearly...*

* * * * * *

Oh? I woke up in the outer perimeter, in a place far and unknown to me as ancient Earth: Anarchia. *Where was I? Who were these people surrounding me?* I got up to have a check-out of surroundings. *Wait, I see buildings, long destroyed.* Bricks malformed beyond their kilns. Streets, once paved with the glory of active civilisation, now empty and wanting for attention. There were primitives all around me, warming themselves up with makeshift hearths to keep the cold out. They gazed not at me. They were too busy about themselves. Buildings without windows surrounded me with a presence. The primitives were huddled in masses, and formed shades of loneliness, as lines of discomfort crossed their faces. Their eyes nearly hidden behind dirt-scarred coverings. They looked like Bedouin tribes from the old days, and surviving just as keenly.

They were of a nomadic, but human nature; something about them made me feel sad for their plight. They were the distant people descended from the ruins of civilisation and yet, they still carried on, as if nothing happened to them recently. I further noted a dimly lit street twisted and turned on a winding road. Drab, like a woman's housecoat. I looked through a window of one of the buildings. There was a woman who lived in a Spartan-styled home, decorated with a plaque of the area she lives in, with its own motto. I could not make out what it said, for the dust and chipping of time occupied the same space. From the open window, I saw her cleaning plain coloured walls, and watering what plants were left that her husband rescued from outside, when the plants tried to grow. She then turned her attention to putting away the dishes, making the beds and cleaning the floors with a vacuum.

She tried to make a meal, but got distracted by the one-station radio blaring out signs of morality and music; a makeshift cacophony, I figured. There were no station markers outside, but I guessed there was someone who found a radio among the ruins and tried to do their best with it. Tiredness overtook her, so she made a cup of tea and looked outside. There was silence and foreboding in her neighbourhood, revealing cars that flew (when they could) and buses that creep along like caterpillars (if there were enough people wanting the service). The buildings were great hulks in the ground, their extensions eating away into one another. Their white-washed frames couldn't win a beauty contest, much less the architecture. Everything looked so monotonous, yet there was a glimmer of hope in all this nonsense.

Someone took me inside one of the intact buildings, and gave me water. I drank it and thanked the fellow in rags, looking like an automaton. The primitives were in a trance-like state, like zombies to think for themselves, little that they had. They did know how to survive and their sense of being was quite different from my own.

They looked a mess; rags of once-fashionable clothing covered their bodies, and the remnants of once-expensive shoes ended their lineage of pride. *Did they last this long since the Blast? How many generations of primitives lived their lives, out here in the deserted city?* You could create a mini-society within these ruins of Man, as the primitives walked through warfare without getting a shot. Oh, if Dad only saw this; if Silage was subject to this, I'd wonder. There was something to be said, if he were here. After all, he'd studied the ancient Irish, and I doubt if they were no different from these people I came across now. Probably better off because they were no better than the olden century of long ago.

Suddenly, I heard a man reading out something; favours, perhaps? He looked smart, as his voice and demeanour was like that of a TV game show host of the 20th century. *Reckoned he had the better rags.* Why? I guess this group had to start over somehow, and it took a lot of guts to see how far they'd come. The man was about my father's age, give or take a year. Smart looking, and figured he was the leader of this pack of humanity. I turned my glimpse away from him, as I looked around, and walked to a window. It was one of the few left intact, looking out at what was a great city. *Old Chicago.*

I ran out the place I stayed at and searched for a better option. *Why did Dad send me here?* Why do it alone, when Silage could be of use? In fact, it would have been better if he sent *both* of us on this survivalist field trip! *Wait a moment... oh damn, yuck, Silage, being with Silage.* With his knowledge of trickery, I would be doubtful if we'd make it. We could make it, but I didn't wish to indulge such a delusion.

I took another breath, ingesting pale air, and stewed gently by the great corporation that was the sun. It knocked the bilge out of me, I tell you! It trickled out of various nimbus clouds, and the entire area looked ominous. Not stormy ominous, but just boring-old-society ominous.

I walked away from all that, and carried on my journey with the clothes on my back, and a burden in my heart. A burden, due to what would come of me. *Would I make it?* Looking out at the small conclaves of primitives gathered around the stone fire, I wondered if they'd let me in on it? *What was their story?* I would never try to guess. Their story played out like a passion play of old. Silage would know about *that.* It was pretty cold by now, after some hours passed, and my clothing was starting to fray from the sun, exposing my skin. *Was I becoming one of them? Would they let me in, or lock me out of their world?*

I tried to be friendly, as if it were the only way to survive. I smiled. They did not. They had no reason to, but did not harass me either. The primitives gathered around a campfire, cooking something in a huge solid pot. This would not be a fun overnight hike for me. This was what Dad had wanted to teach to me, but could not, because of his studies and fine conditions at home. He would *never* resort to this. I would not be surprised if he were sent by his father out here to live among the current tribal peoples of Anarchia. I guessed that was why he chose science instead, and drove his nose straight into it; he never got this pleasure. Being wishful about flight was a bad move for me, despite me wanting to pursue it, along with possible exploration. I regretted the argument with Dad when he called me up on it, and he shut me down. I didn't hate him for it, but the feeling burned me inside. I had to end up with primitives, and live like them to be taught a life-lesson, whatever *that* was.

The primitives started to dish out their food, and everyone had a bowl ready. They chose to remain where they were, until...

'Would you like some dinner?'

I spun round to see a young woman, offering her assistance, and cried out, 'You speak?'

'Yes, I do, duh. Why not?'

Why not, indeed?

'Nobody else does,' I observed.

'You're a stranger,' she explained. 'You are not one of us, despite your look.' She pointed at my near-threadbare clothing.

I sniggered about it. 'Yeah, I could use a decent suit and some food. I'll take you up on your offer. Is your place far?'

'Nah,' she led me toward a large building that was once a bank. 'I've got a stew on in my place, one of the other ladies is watching it for me. This food is for the group that you see huddled. We live in groups, and come together when the Leader, Master Barkhor, shows up with favours, and helps us out some.'

'I believe I've seen him. What were you doing out here?'

'Ah, fetching more wood for the fire, as the saying went, once upon a time, like.'

I laughed again. This one was full of humour. Like Twiki, but better. She was human. She was a girl. My age. Yum.

CHAPTER IX

She lived alone. Her place was in a bank, once removed. A next door job, with a tiller at the back. She occupied the space. Others did, too, but she didn't live *with* them exactly. The place was very tired in decor, and found its way into a dust pile. It looked like it'd been a burnt out hulk, made cosy by the primitives that lived here. A makeshift home for a makeshift time. *What would they think of next?* However, it made for a small community, and for them, I guessed it worked.

I rubbed my hands at the fire set-up she had, while the stew was still in the making. I recalled it took a lot to make a stew, and Silage would ramble on about it during his time reading about old Ireland. The pot started to billow steam. *Ummm, ummm*, I was looking forward to tasting the stew. Maybe Silage had something there after all. It would hearken back for him, and his studies would become more enlivening, as he'd be 'eating' the past. *At least I beat him to it!* I thrilled in the excitement that I could surpass my brother at something, even if I had to transport my way out of New Chicago to do it.

I thought it dignified to introduce myself. 'I'm Elias Huer. What's your name?'

'Cindihan O'Myde. Nice to meet you.'

'How do you do, Cindihan?' I shook her hand, realising something special.

A flicker of light took hold in my mind. I looked at her again, and wondered. My twin wasn't horsing about the legend after all. The legend of Muffyhuer and Cindihan was alive in the 25th century! I was Huer (certainly not Muffy), and she was Cindihan. This really threw me for a loop, as now I had something in common *with* Silage, but better. *I met Cindihan. Who did Silage meet up with at that Draconian school of his???* I felt so smug, just thinking about it.

Still, I had to be sure, but not persistently obvious. I did not want to be overbearing about it, so I trod carefully when asking. The girl looked a bit jittery, as if to run away from things. I saw no reason for her to run away from me, but who was to say?

I tried to make conversation, as she got the stew all ready and waiting to eat. 'Been here long?'

'Since the grandparents died, I took over my own life here,' she said, 'I help out and it makes it easier without them bearing down on you every so often.'

She served me some stew, and muddled within herself. She seemed very agitated, but had a playfulness about her. I frowned at the conditions she lived in. I felt worse that her reference to grandparents had negative connotations. It looked like it was up to *me* to set her straight.

So I postulated, 'Would you like to live elsewhere, if you could?'

She pondered and wandered around her mind, a bit. 'Eh, I've got everything here. The man out there called Barkhor makes announcements and helps us out. A peddler of necessity, he is. The competition could be ferocious, but the grandparents allotted for my care in their wills. Sparse care, nothing more. He finds his sources and attains them for assistance. That's all I know. I guess that's all that matters. He put us in groups and we aid one another in all things.'

She turned away, moping some. I put down my bowl to cuddle her. 'That's why you're so thin.'

'It's not just day-to-day living, I try to run around and get exercise in this dump. Kind of hard though, when you have everybody looking at you.'

I was surprised that even in this ghastly state, there was time for 'exercise'.

'Yes,' I reflected, 'But your name, do you know it has an ancient connection?'

'Cindihan, wife of Muffyhuer, fallen under the great town of Oconnalow grand-daughter of what society called the O'Mydes. Yes, I've heard the story. People talk. People know their own legends around here, and name one another after their favourites. The grandparents and myself were reminders of what everyone else knew of the legend. It seemed as if we were incarnations of those characters, and despite the difficulty of pronouncing their Germanic-sounding crap name, as the primitives called it, society referred to them as the O'Mydes, and myself being dear Cindihan. It was the closest the primitives got to some connection with the past, possibly their own. The grandparents hated it, but they had no choice but to bend to the will of those around them to survive. My real mother and father died long ago, and I was cared for by the grandparents. They weren't well-liked in the community, though they alluded that they were. Personally, I think it was an illusion in and of itself, but there you are.'

The was a long pause between us. 'I'm used to Cindihan, or Cindy though, and most people have nothing against me. They all knew it was the grandparents that were the problem. There are no grudges or anything like that. People have been understanding toward me, but it is difficult to deal with such a burdensome experience.'

'Okay', I muttered, not expecting such a lengthy backstory describing a heritage of bad experience. 'You'll do as you are.' I dared not ask about her past any further. I liked her as she was.

We ate more stew. 'This is really good,' I bantered on.

'Thanks, I'm glad you like it. I never had much company. Everyone knows one another here, and outsiders are a rarity in these parts.'

'In any parts,' I concluded.

'Done. Yeah.'

I smirked, 'So I'm it, eh?'

'Yeah, you are.'

She was in her early twenties, brown eyes, golden hair, definitive sides attractive, as well as a smallish face that weathered well in these times. Her dress was something out of a messy drawer, but I didn't mind. We were all messy, somewhat.

She then offered, 'Want anything else?'

'No, no. I'm fine.'

I was most satisfied, knowing where I could get a spare meal, if I needed one, in this semi-hostile community.

'I'll go and clear these up, shall I?' Cindy reached for the dishes and put them near a makeshift sink to clean them. Guess it wasn't all bad in Anarchia; some semblance of order was retained. But, sadly, not by many. I was lucky to be able to find this fledgling community, out here in the sticks of barrenness. I didn't feel like I wanted to be a part of it though, I doubt Cindy did either. The primitives looked like they were stuck in their own ways, not necessarily in the past, but a nuanced primitiveness emerged from this folk. In another world, this would be charming. In this ravaged one, well, I don't know.

I looked around, where she made her section of an old bank lobby hospitable, along with the few others that lived with her. It was obvious it was 'every man for himself' around here, but I can see some bonding, if necessary. Poor Cindy was left to her own; yet, she did look after herself quite well, at least. *That was a keen attribute that I would never fault.*

When she returned, I wanted to broach the subject of boyfriends, so I asked, 'Have you anybody around?'

She stared at me innocently. 'Who would I have?'

'I don't know. A nice girl like you, you know, going out and all.'

She certainly got the message. 'Ah, that. Nah, no favours, no boys, if that's what you're on about. Everyone here is an acquaintance of mine, nothing more. Like I told you, the grandparents saw to it that I'd be cared for after they'd gone, but there were no provisions for any day in the beyond. Besides, you do not get close when you don't know if you'd live the next day.'

'Right,' I sighed. I definitely got haunted by her last sentence and showed concern.

So she clarified it for me. 'Living in these conditions. They're not bad, overall. I mean it is not the toll-house mansion of yore, is it?'

I quickly understood. 'I see.'

'I mean, it's not ideal, is it? Not the best, but not exactly the worst.'

'No, it's not,' I agreed.

'But you have to call it home to survive.'

I wanted to curse my father so badly for sending me out here. I already cursed Silage for his good fortune. I imbibed in distaste at being out here, but I confess I was lucky to be talking to Cindy. She was not something I bargained for, and doubtful that she would be the outcome that Dad or Silage would be looking for. I did not care a wink, because I got to love her company. It was better than being gas-stricken alone out here.

'You don't have to like it here, I guess,' Cindy added. 'You come from the other side, and show it in your personality.'

'No, I don't like it,' I boldly declared. 'I enjoyed the stew, and I find it admirable what you'd done here, but, *damn*. Where I come from, nobody lives like *this*.'

'So much for the spoils,' she said cryptically, 'It's all we do, it's all we know. We're trapped here. I see you could do better and have done so.'

I had done better. 'But I want to take you away from here.'

'Try it; there's nothing to stop you,' she dared me.

'Good luck with that,' a burnt-skinned lady blurted out, collecting scraps off the floor. 'I bet you'd be back in time for breakfast. Get ready for some home-cooking.'

What was this girl living like?

Determined, I made up my mind. 'You and me, we're getting out of here. You and me both.'

Cindy looked at me with those earthen-eyes of hers. Dark, rich, and delicious as coffee on a cold winter's morning, even that of a nuclear winter. This was a nuclear summer that I would never forget. I wondered what it was like here in the winter?

'You heard me, we're getting out of here,' I cried hastily.

She asked, 'What about Arachnia?'

'Wha-,' I paused in horror, 'What about it?'

'It's on the west side. You're in Anarchia,' she explained. 'To leave, you'll have to go through the spidery part called Arachnia.'

Great. In addition to the dirt of this rotten, God-forsaken place, I'd have to juggle with spiders. Or men. Or both. What had I gotten myself in for, and wondered if Silage did any better?

CHAPTER X

I still wondered about my brother, when Cindy came up to me.

'There's a place near here called Dilapidation Mall. We could live there for a time,' she said.

'Well, you're the leader here,' I responded.

We made tracks toward this mall-thing she was going on about. My mind returned to Silage and how he was doing in his education. I could enquire about him, after all, we are not totally incompetent. But then I saw the horrors around me, as I walked westward. There were more primitives about, staring and huddling among themselves. Buildings scarred beyond damage disguised as shelter for them. The damage was extensive, and the people who lived here were no better than the place I met Cindy in. With the little darling beside me, I could not see any distant problems, and I started to like her. The coming destination didn't steer me away from her.

I called aloud anyway, just in case. 'I wonder how Silage is doing?'

She turned to me, 'Silage?'

'Yeah, my brother, Silas. I nicknamed him Silage.'

'You have a brother?'

'Not only that, a twin.'

She squealed, 'Oh, there are *two* of you! Wouldn't that be fun?'

'Come on, it's not like that,' I smirked in my stride. 'He's not *that* exciting but you never know. He's in school, still, on Dracos.'

'That is interesting,' Cindy went, then back-stepped, 'Wait, why do you call him Silage?'

'If you met him, you'll see why,' I joked.

I hoped he made out okay, I thought, as my feet tread the once gloried pavement of old. Now, it was all crumbly rock that went muddy in the rain. It was a frivolous thought, thinking about Silage, compared to the monumental task at hand: survival. I looked around me, seeing places where business models of yesteryear didn't work any more. Everything was thrown into dust. With Cindy at my side, we moved on. The weather got warmer, as we moved outward from the city. It wasn't all that bad, and it reminded me of the Wild West of old. It fascinated me, thinking about it. It did help me understand Silage's historical interest. But I, well, I was *living* the history, even though in another century. *Now, that was cool!*

'Maybe we could settle here for the night,' Cindy suggested, 'Seems duly romantic, no?'

'Sure, my dear,' I cooed fondly at her, 'Let's get settled, where all the rattlesnakes slither.'

She sensed the tease, but giggled, because I did it so well; but then a real rattlesnake appeared.

Mockingly, I went, 'Hi, Silage.'

I giggled, too, when the snake answered me, 'Sssseellloooo.'

I nearly jumped out of my skin.

'It talks,' she shrieked.

'I do talk, sssssommeewhat,' it said, 'It'sssss eeevoluuuution, after your ffaaallll.'

I wasn't in the mood for this. No one could have survived the Big Blast, not even lower life forms. Yet, who was I to argue? Life could have conceived again, creating raucous monsters such as this entity I was 'talking' to. As we evolved into higher, and smarter beings, perhaps animal life did too. *Silage would have a field day with him, no doubt!* It would be a conversation worth eavesdropping in on.

'Let us be,' I commanded, 'We're not in your way.'

'I know,' the snake predicted, rattling its slimy tail. 'Your brother will be a grrreeat leader sssssomeedaaaayy. You will be grrreeat in your own laaand.'

My own land? 'What are you talking about?'

'You'll sssseeeee,' it slithered down a path, until it sped out of sight. Probably found a rodent to eat or something. Snake-talk never lasts long anyway. You would not want to talk long, as it usually ended badly for the talker, even if it was another snake. Both of them would battle it out and one would win, devouring the other. *Ewh.* I was ever thankful I lived in New Chicago, but wondered about Silage's and my predicted future greatness. I kept that to myself and kept on the journey.

I reflected on the background that surrounded us. 'I don't think that was much of a conversation, do you?'

'I dunno,' Cindy whispered, 'Do you talk to creatures very often?'

I smiled at her. 'No, I don't. I have an ancestor called Amber Daye, who once had a conversation with a snake. Then he killed it.'

'Eeewwhh,' she made a face. 'How uncivilised.'

'How indeed, but I was pleased to let him go. I've no gun. Amber did, and used it when he had to.'

'But that snake wasn't much different than the one your fella came across.'

'Yes, but our time is different. Maybe the snake was right in this.'

She suddenly became interested in the topic. 'How so?'

'Well,' I paused, not trying to sound silly over it. 'We suffered the Big Blast, right?'

'Yes.'

'So, there were survivors. Survivors beget survivors, that is to say, children. Now, these children grow up, different, but no different than in the past. They just grow up with new ideas, new surroundings, new life codes.'

'Ah. So this snake is no better than we are?'

'No he isn't,' I grinned at her. 'He is no better than any other life form on the planet. We're starting again. So are they. So are any other bugs, mammals, birds, insects, and the like.'

'Wow,' she reflected on what I said.

We went toward a small patch, where there was what was left of a mall. The building remained intact, but the innards were gone. Hobos made homes there, naturally, and I felt it was best to be moving on.

I checked my baggage and cried out, 'You have over soaked my thermos! Look at all this devastation,' I moaned, nearly weeping, 'This used to be one among many shopping districts. All gone.'

'You don't have to go on about it. Do you not think I am aware of the problems out here? And your thermos is not over soaked.'

She took my thermos container and wiped off the excess and tried to give hope to me. 'Dilapidation Mall is one of the main hubs of post-Blast civilisation, the remains of what was,' Cindy explained, 'I heard it's like a paradise in there, if you know where to look. That is what I'd heard anyway from the others I was living with.'

'Paradise among survivors? Not likely,' I scorned. 'It's up to you to know the light side from darkness.'

I dragged my feet in the continual dirt. Cindy ventured off like a girl in a crazy white dress. Yet, she was not wearing a dress. She was wearing a jumpsuit this time, patchworked to conceal unnecessary holes worn through over time.

'Arachnia feels far from here,' she noted, 'I hope we reach that Mall first.'

'Yeah,' I remarked, 'A good thing too. I don't want spiders at my heels.'

'Well, if snakes could talk, imagine what spiders could do.'

I stopped dead in my tracks in fear. 'Now don't you start.'

'I'm not. I was just postulating.'

'Go postulate somewhere else, then,' I dismissed.

At this point, a swarm of spiders of all sorts gathered momentum towards us. My mind raced a marathon it hadn't seen in years. Furry, leggy and eyeballing us intensely, they crawled about, try to surround us to prevent escape.

'Run, Cindy,' I yelled.

She went off, and realised the spiders were everywhere, without relent.

'Elias, Elias,' she screamed.

And I wasn't doing any better. I pulled away, narrowly escaping, when I reached her. 'Come on, just a bit more.'

I held my hand out to her, but it was too late. The spiders effected their target and they had us.

'You cannot escape the Crystal Webb,' they shouted. 'You are now part of it. You will be encapsulated within our prime spawn.'

I screamed, being stung unconscious, as they took Cindy away from me to Arachnia. As it turned out, Arachnia wasn't far from here, either. It was conveniently located nearby the Dilapidation Mall, which was no longer a paradise, as Cindy thought, but a more sinister complex.

CHAPTER XI

The Crystal Webb, I later learned, *was* the old Dilapidation Mall, before Arachnia had taken it over. Bound up and gagged, I felt I was going through a long dark tunnel. It was not a tunnel that looked familiar; stinging with barrenness and crawling with insectoids of all kinds. The Arachnids were the most dominant here, but allowed other species to manifest and feed themselves. It was not wise to hoard everything, and as the insect world was starting over, they needed a place to begin. *And why not here? It seemed a good a place as any.* All sorts of multi-legged creatures came alive in this new dump of what was a main centre of commerce for humans. The devastation was brutal here, after the Blast. It was no wonder they called this place Dilapidation Mall. *It looked like cold storage from the past.*

When the old shops, that once gave this place a good name, stood proud and firm, were now lined with spider webs, cocoons, and bodies from which they ate. It was not a saleable project on offer. I couldn't believe Cindy thought this would be *paradise*. It might have been, a long time ago, or she believed the ever-changing memories of people she'd lived with, who didn't know any better, and thought otherwise. Maybe they wanted to see a better place and make-do with what was there. They wanted to bring optimism, when in reality it was not there.

When I awoke from the reverie, I stood up, still bound, but they took the gag off me for questioning. In a corner, I saw Cindy was stitched up in a comatose state, blinded, keeping her still. *Probably just like her childhood. All bound up and gagged. Oooh!* Against the wall, victims were being consumed in countless webs around them. *Closing in. Suffocating them.* I didn't want to think about it.

A voice shrilled sharply. 'You are from New Chicago?'

I spun around, focusing my attention on an overgrown... spider! I wished I had a gun like Amber did. *I would truly know the meaning of defence.*

'Elias Huer, son of the fabled Doctor. A genius in all things. Too bad his son didn't turn out much better,' the voice continued. 'I am Eri-Cast, Leader of Arachnia.'

'I think I did pretty good so far,' I fought the spasm to attack. 'How did you know who I am?'

'I just do. We spiders are most resourceful. We relish in knowing who we have, so we can merge their intelligence with ours. This will make us more powerful in the area. We eventually plan to take over Anarchia. We've tried, but the humans there are most resilient. For now, yes. For ever, we'll see,' Eri-Cast giggled.

I yelled out, 'What did you do to Cindihan?'

'I think you'll find her... comfortable. She's in a cell, blinded, and will fall off the chasm one day, so to speak; unless she somehow manages to free herself from the spell, which is unlikely. Or *you* plan a rescue. Pah!'

I got impatient with the multi-legged being. Though relatively good-looking and dark, for a spider, his demeanour creeped me out. 'Look she's been through enough already. Take me.'

'No. We do not like your kind, preferring to work on the females of the species. Any species. You will remain until you outlive your usefulness to us.'

I challenged him, like my brother in days of old. 'And what kind of usefulness is that?'

The Leader didn't deign to give me an answer, and left the room quietly. He left me so suddenly, that I was speechless.

Like all Leaders, he was a not senseless bog animal, but obviously saw silence was the best option for *himself.* It was okay for Eri-Cast to walk out on me, but not okay if I did it to *him. Oh, excuse me!* It was made perfectly clear that even captors of another century did not act any differently from the past ones. They all stayed on the prey, until they weren't hungry any more, or information was not being fed to them properly. Then there was a great bother as to what to do with a prisoner. Here in Arachnia, the message proved ominous.

With Cindy still pinned to the wall, delusional and blind, I sunk my head in my hands, trying to figure a way out of here. This Dilapidation Mall paradise was now a long way off, and now I was thinking of going back to New Chicago, bringing Cindy with me and starting afresh. I felt helpless within this multi-ridden chamber of horrors. It was clean, though, but filthy in its purpose. Eri-Cast didn't look scary as such, but his face had a webbed effect on it, the dark, hairy eight legs completing his purpose in life. He looked humanoid but otherworldly. It left a ghastly hole in the meaning of existence.

I was left on my own for some time. I looked around, and found the exit point. I jumped at the chance, and found a small folding knife in my pocket that released my binds, when I was zapped by a laser, and taped to a web that was plastered to the door.

'You can't escape, son,' Eri-Cast announced over the tannoy, 'You will be put in stasis, like your girlfriend here.'

'Oh yeah,' I threatened, 'What makes you so sure of my prowess?'

'No one could escape a web without being eaten.'

I hated this, and wondered if there was any hope. I looked around the room to see other people, like Cindihan, enmeshed as web fodder, in various stages.

'Insects are *so* disgusting,' I spat out, with snake-like venom.

Who now was becoming a creature?

Eri-Cast overheard me. 'We think you humans are more disgusting, and destructive. You've destroyed your own world.'

'Not completely,' I called back, thinking of cities like New Chicago, New Phoenix, New London.

'We can make it ours,' the Leader laughed. 'I've already taken over what you people refer to as Dilapidation Mall.'

Sounds a bit like Silage, don't you think?

I ignored the damn bug and carried out my way of escape. *Yet, I had no way.* I refused to sit idle, though, and Eri-Cast was counting on that. He figured the more I peruse the scene, the more fun it will be to watch me escape the impossible. So *he* says. But, *didn't scientists work with the impossible?* I used everything I was taught by Dad, long ago in his lab, and all the schooling I had so far. It was obvious I was being put to the test. I was never overborne by family, like Cindihan was, so I felt an inner strength, well within me. I figured Eri-Cast would make it difficult to spin through those spidery webs of his, the Crystal Webb effect. I passed it by in thought, and got on with escaping, soon freeing myself from my web on the door.

Alternatively, I found it hurtful Dad let me go out into this forsaken wilderness in the first place. I figured he'd have no way of knowing. No one knew what was out here. Only communication between inner cities, like New Chicago or New Phoenix, were known, and cherished considering the monies society poured out for everyone to keep in touch. Outer cities like Arachnia or Anarchia for that matter, were driven into the dust they became.

But I found Cindihan in that dust. You weren't going to take her for a fool to live there forever. Even she deserved better. Everyone did. *But I found her*. And I wanted to give her that chance. She seemed like an okay kid, deep down, as womanhood was near approaching. Or will, if we get out of this mess. I knew Silage would have a real laugh over Eri-Cast. *He might even join him, if he could.* Loyal or not, I wouldn't put it past him.

I went back to Cindy to see if anything changed, and if there was a way to dismantle the gunk that lay around her. She was just lying upright, still and alone. I pinched her to see if she reacted.

'Owww,' she cried.

I went official. 'Cindihan?'

'Elias, is that you?'

The Arachnids hadn't gotten to her yet.

'It is. Can you get down from there?'

She moved her hand to wipe off the fuzz that was emerging from her webby existence. She saw my fair face, blue eyes, and wanting mouth.

'I think so,' she fidgeted around to free herself. The web was too strong, so I helped her. *Nothing.*

Eri-Cast found this amusing from afar, and taunted us the whole time, as he was studying our moves distinctly. His laughter prevented further hilarity on our part. He didn't speak any further, and silently watched us. We moved around like insects on our own. He found us amusing specimens, and wished for further display of our temperament.

I asked, 'You okay in there?'

'Yeah, I think so. This web is sticky, can you remove it?'

'I'm trying.' I looked on the floor to see if there was rubble of any kind. Pity, spiders are clean and Eri-Cast's lair did not look like a city dump. So, it looked like I had to use more of my mind and strength this time, to get her out. I had the knife still, and took it out and used it upon the web. I loosened some string, which was tethered to the greater web. I suddenly got the damn thing sorted when I instructed Cindy.

'When I count to three, you pull yourself out, understand?'

'Okay,' she said.

I ran my hands down the web to check for any weak points. *Damn, these things were solid. Wait a minute. I think I...*

'Hold on,' I urged, as I found a small area to work from. 'You'll have to move as I release the web, yeah?'

She did so, and I gave her the knife to hold on to. She put it in her pocket, and gave me a 'thank you' kiss.

She was finally freed from that vermin wasteland, and I wanted to free the others who looked unconsumed. They were here longer than Cindy, and I felt to leave well enough alone. It didn't look good for them. We ran toward an exit point, before going through the Mall itself, with its stretchy, winding paths. I had no reason to hestitate, the meaning was clear. I cast my lot with Cindihan, and we ran out of the webby labyrinth Mall together. The walls were caked in webs, and smaller spiders spat out at the sides. The old shops that had webbed walls and fittings got grosser by the minute. We went toward an old escalator to go to another level. Soon, we were running from other insectoids, as well as the multi-legged kind. Centipedes loved it here; they enjoyed the *splatulas* the humans left behind. The splatulas were primitive fly-swatters, but used for the reverse purpose, even so named by one of the centipedes. It was a horrible sight, and we didn't hesitate to spend time there. *We definitely wanted out.*

CHAPTER XII

However, the Leader Eri-Cast had other ideas, and noticed our movements. Spiders had a good sense when it came to sight. Other bugs had their own specialities, but I cared not to think about them. I didn't like to think they had the upper leg, as they'd put it. I guess that was why Cindy got entangled. Yet, she was still intact, untouched by Arachnian wiles.

'Going so soon,' he said to us, pausing with a breath to eat something crawling near him. 'There's no escape for you two.'

He tried to catch us personally, like a permanent invitation to lunch. It would have passed as a decent time, but unfortunately for Eri-Cast, we declined his RSVP.

'We're going back to where we belong,' I glared back. 'We will not stay here with you and your *bugs*.'

'Oh? Getting a little species-centred, are we? And where is that place you so long to return to,' the snarling continued, flashing white specks of teeth. His mind started to penetrate mine, and soon he knew where we were heading to. 'New Chicago?'

Ewh, I wasn't getting formal with this fellow. I reached for a nearby... something, and threw it at the Leader. *No disrespect, of course.*

'You will be dessert,' the Leader's grasp caught unto me, but Cindy helped free me. She found some oddball gadget laying around in her pocket, and gave it to me. *That knife. How handy!*

She shouted, 'Come on Elias!'

I freed myself from the evil grasp, and we fled hastily through a long-winded chamber. It was harsh as hell, but we knew we'd make it.

'Well, well,' Eri-Cast mused, as he called in his guards. 'Seize them, I'm still hungry, lest you be my lunch.'

The guardsmen went after us, in a telling manner. They crouched and scurried along, going from wall to wall with extending limbs and hyper-sensitive eyesight. They tried to capture us again, but we were too swift this time.

Eri-Cast spoke after us on his vibromitter. 'Is it you can't stand Old Chicago?'

I wanted to yell out, NO, but kept fleeing.

The cackling taunts continued, 'What your kind once had, dwelling in a vainglorious state, showing superiority over all creatures? Showing all your powers in the universe? What you used to be?'

Used to be. Yeah right. We've come very far since the Blast and never will we stop progressing toward the universe. *If we could conquer it, too.* We were most capable of that, but then there was the stickiness of social situations. Meeting those of newer cultures than ours. Oh, that would be a good plan, *if.*

I stopped thinking about that, as soon my mentality was one with Eri-Cast. *No, I cannot do that!* I had to resist the fellow. So, I reflected on Silage. Yes, he could conquer the universe himself, after all he was *in* it. On a distant planet called Dracos. Well, I wonder how he'd fair against Eri-Cast, Leader of Arachnia. *I'd bet he'd cast his lot with him and join in*, I thought again. Actually, the idea wasn't a bad one, but seeing him within a spidery mess was a long shot. Gross even. The main question was, *would he put up with the Crystal Webb or be stuck in it forever?* Still.

I had nothing more to say to or about that spidery leader. I concentrated more on escaping his clutches. I looked around, as I ran to see if there was anything I could use to ease it. Those guards were getting closer. My pockets were already invaded by the young Cindihan, and she still had my knife.

I called to her, 'You still have that knife?'

She stumbled a bit, feeling her own pockets. 'You've got it.'

Ah yes. I grabbed the item out; we stopped and crouched behind a large rock. I fiddled with the knife, as it had another purpose. There was a ticking sound emerging.

'Lay down,' I ordered, as I threw it into the air.

The device went off, and smoke billowed out from a tiny outlet. The guards gagged and fell down.

I took back the knife, once the smoke died down, as we headed for our exit point. I was in no mood to scurry around with Eri-Cast again. He was suave, but detrimentally gross. Life was full of villainy, along with kindness, and right now, I would rather stick with kindness.

The outdoors seemed a long time away from us, but we made it. The sun was high, but on the decline.

'It's afternoon. Let's go back to your place,' I suggested.

'Okay. I thought we were leaving.'

'Yeah, I did too.'

I soon lamented my decision, but for the moment, it would have to do. I got to like Cindy and enjoy her company. We didn't do anything personal together, yet, but I had a suspicion she would be my girl for the long haul.

* * * * *

We walked for several long hours until an odd vehicle approached. We were at our limit, and she was about to faint from the blazing heat. The vehicle had markings of ancient lineage. It was identified as being from Old Chicago. *Who knew a 20th century vehicle could run in the distant future?*

A man sat at the helm, beckoning us to come in. The man with the favours the blazen-ass Master Barkhor.

'Thought you might need a ride back,' he said, 'What were you doing out here?'

'Long story. We ran into Arachnians,' I answered.

'Oh, miserable people. Those they capture are left without senses.'

'I'll say. Cindy had a slight brush with that, 'til I got her out. Then she helped me. Why are you out here?'

Barkhor smiled. 'How do you think we survive? I scrounge for meagre rations. Supplies left in the rubble could be useful.'

'But they're contaminated with nuclear dust,' I gasped.

'Ah, but I found a way to neutralise the acid in order for these items to become useful to us. Just because you're covered in dust doesn't make you unviable,' he explained, as he started the engine again, as it timed-out during our conversation. 'You can always clean yourself off.'

We scurried on, in the minute vehicle when soon, we were back at Anarchia. We were dropped off by the old bank where Cindy lived.

'Thanks much,' I waved to Barkhor.

'In order to survive out here, I'm willing to help out. For Cindihan, I'd bend over backwards. It's part of the will.'

I smiled.

'You do not know what will happen if I don't,' he added.

I had an idea. 'So can I take the girl back to my home in New Chicago?'

'Well, let's see how much you want to take her.'

I didn't think I'd have a match with this one. 'Is she on raffle or something?'

'No, but I do have to uphold her grandparents' intention.'

'But you can negate it, and free yourself from responsibility for her. Who is to enforce it?'

He muttered, 'Maybe. We'll take this up later. There is much to do here.'

We left his vehicle; he sped on. *The prize wasn't won, yet.* We walked back, past the dumpsters teeming with possible resources that people used when desperate. The old buildings still looked old and worn. Dust lay on the street like rubble and that woman in the house I saw when I first arrived here, still did her routines. I did not know where all this would take me, though and it singed me to think of this existence as nothing but intolerable. But, if we took these people, with Cindy, back to New Chicago, *how would they cope? Would the ease of life make them merrier, or something to take advantage of?* I figured there will be other times, and more chances to take Cindy back from the clutches of a family long dead, and as dead as Anarchia itself.

CHAPTER XIII

Meanwhile, Cindy found her 'hovel' and scampered inside. The place was run-down as ever, and other members of the community living there stayed by the small fire they built. She removed the yuck-covered clothing she'd worn earlier, to erase the memory of it, and threw it on the fire. She got a dress from an oblong dresser and put it on. Actually, it was a smock, and not something you'd want to be seen dead in at the ball.

'Long time no see,' one of the nameless people called out. I was sure they had a name, but cared not to enquire about it.

'Hi,' Cindy greeted.

'There is some sandwiches over there if you're hungry. Where've you been, girl?'

'Arachnia.'

The lady's eyes flew open. 'Arachnia? Isn't that where the spider-people live?'

'Uh-huh, and other bugs too. They've got lots of them. They even took over Dilapidation Mall,' she nodded, grabbing a sandwich. It had been a long while since we last ate. She did not dare tell them about Eri-Cast and his crazy schemes.

'Well I'll be. That's too bad. I've heard stories that there were some folk down there trying to etch a living like we are,' the lady replied, and went off to do some cleaning up.

Well, I knew what happened to such folk. I approached Cindy, and gave her a kiss. She gave me a part of her sandwich.

'Thanks,' I said, kissing her some more.

'Oooh, Cindy's got a boyfriend,' the others giggled.

'Well, I wouldn't say that,' she went all bashful.

'You're kissing, ain't ya?'

'We've been through a lot together,' Cindy explained.

She looked at me, as I ate the rest of the sandwich she gave me. The other people there moved on with themselves, as I got cosy with Cindy. I became more fond of her and working together, we grew a tad closer. It was a nice feeling.

I asked her, 'Do you really want to remain here, or go elsewhere?'

'I did wish to leave sometime', she said, 'I did have a chat with Master Barkhor and he said we can talk about it later. I doubt he'd concede to you.'

'Nawh, I think he will. I've planned it so he will hand you over to me.'

Her brown eyes widened. 'Like a prize jackpot?'

I sniggered, 'That is you, ain't it?'

'I didn't think you'd think so highly of me. Nobody did before.'

Her head hung down and she became sad. I cuddled her and gave her a hug. 'I do think highly of you. Your actions in Arachnia spoke volumes to me. In fact...,' I stopped to give her another kiss.

She gave me a smile and another kiss on the cheek. I wanted more, though, but didn't want to pressure her. We snuggled into a fast sleep soon after.

The next day, I awoke to the dump reality set us in. No wonder she was talking of leaving! She had already been up for some time, probably helping the others with morning duties. I lay there watching, but feeling guilty as this was a community thing. Helping out was all part of it, even if you were not officially so. Soon, I noticed something nice was cooking. It smelled good. I looked in the pot. Grit-like porridge.

My sarcasm knew no bounds. 'Oooh,' I mimed eagerly, 'Can I have some?'

A lady by the pot gave me a bowl. 'Help yourself. Then you can help the others, and clean up after yourself. The sink is over there.'

She pointed out where the sink was, and walked away, doing more chores. It seemed like she relished in this sort of work.

I began to eat, and thank God I *could* survive in this mess of a society. At least it *was* a society, save for New Chicago. No one from there knows what's out here and their snobbery dictates it so. I can see why Dad made me come out here. As a scientist, he saw the nature of things, and things that were unexplored, had to be ascertained. If not, everything becomes an unknown, and he didn't like that. Problem was, I wished I could contact him somehow, to show him I'm alright. Inviting Cindy, would be the least of my worries. She was so pliable. She left me to help with dishes, and clean-up duties. She fed late stragglers, and proved herself to be hard-working.

'Your turn to eat now,' another woman came up to her. 'I'll take over from here.'

'Thanks,' she said.

Cindy finally got the break from her work-time to eat, and helped herself to a nice bowl of slop. *Well, okay, it was tasty slop.*

I looked at her. 'You alright, girl? You look a mess.'

'Ummm-ummm,' she responded with a mouthful of beautiful, slimming porridge. Slimming in the sense that you just want one bowl and be done with it. 'You can be a mess when you work hard at something.'

'I wish mornings would be just us,' I pondered aimlessly, 'No running around doing things, feeding others. Just being ourselves, with ourselves, to ourselves.'

'Yeah,' Cindy agreed, 'It'd be great to wake up in the morning with just you around. No one else, no one who needs help. Nothing. Just us.'

'I'd like that with you, Cindihan.'

'Me too, Elias.'

We sighed in our overdrawn comfort. She finished her bowl of food and went to the sink and washed it off. A thank you was murmured to her in acknowledgement. It was good, as people needed to pick themselves up off the floor and get moving.

'I can see why you wanted to leave,' I stated.

'I know you're probably itching to return to your home, too. Probably so clean and simple. Pretty, with breathtaking sights, large buildings, powered vehicles of all sorts.'

'With you, everything's powered.' I kissed her. 'New Chicago is a much nicer, organised, and cleaner place. Healthy living, like here, but again, cleaner. You'd love it.'

She continued to help the others, and pitched in with further washing, when I looked at my watch and realised I had that meeting with Master Barkhor.

She came back. I looked concerned about something.

'What is it?'

I sighed. 'Master Barkhor and I will be meeting soon, to discuss you.'

'Me?'

'Yes, you. He's due here shortly.'

'Okay. I know he does make rounds, checks up to see if everybody's okay. Probably will make a quick stop to see how I'm doing.'

I looked at her.

'Part of the contract,' she said.

Oh! That took me by surprise. No one deserves *that*. Those grandparents really had her tied down here. I did not like that. It felt like they were stifling her from the grave and I wanted to change things around here, for good.

She came closer to me. 'Want to help before Barkhor arrives?'

I agreed, and helped out the rest of the folk in her hovel. Some of them were still eating; there was conversation and all-round morale building to feed the minds of the people, never mind their bodies. They looked a happy bunch, but sad, because they lived in this squabble. It was a hard existence, but many here were used to it.

Master Barkhor sounded his vehicle, and pulled up. Everyone gathered around him, as if looking for extra winnings, which he had none. His visitations were the highlight of these people's lives, and they loved him for it. Even if he had nothing to give, but a smile for them. The encouragement allowed them to last beyond their years in this place. And that was enough for these citizens of Anarchia, if you dared to call them that.

He walked through the small crowd, putting his vehicle to stand-by mode. They made room for him, as he entered the portal of the old bank. Everyone in the room fell silent, as he walked toward us. He wished for some privacy, and asked if he could be left be for the moment. The people carried on, doing their thing, while he was doing his, with us.

He then asked, 'So, how are you two getting along?'

'Fine,' I said, in all seriousness. 'Now, what about Cindihan?'

'What about Cindihan? She's a fantastic girl, don't you think?'

'We discussed taking her back to New Chicago with me. She deserves better.'

'With you?'

I stood my ground. 'Yes.'

He looked at Cindy, like a melting parfait in his hand. 'I know she deserves it. Are you willing to wager on her?'

What more do I have to do to get her??

'Wager? I have no money.'

'Who does around here? That's why I pass favours around. It just so happens that Cindihan has a bit of an advantage here…'

'Because of her grandparents' will,' I ended the sentence. 'Yes, I know about that, but now she's of age, can I take her back to New Chicago with me?'

'Will your people accept her?'

'How will they not? I've got a brat for a brother, I'm certain they'll take to the young lady.'

'Well,' he ruffled into his pockets, taking an old coin out. 'Pick a side.'

'Tails,' I called.

'Okay,' he shook the coin in his hands, like a pair of dice and flung it onto the floor.

Thankfully, it landed tails. I won.

'Lucky winner, Elias Huer. You've won the game and you get the girl.'

I was most pleased and I turned to Cindy. 'You're mine now. Happy?'

She answered me with more hugs and kisses.

'That's the biggest prize I've ever given out. She is definitely something else. Something further, you might think.'

'Yeah,' I mused, thinking Anarchia will become a distant memory very soon.

Barkhor went into his pocket and fished out some papers in a folder. He glanced at them. The grandparents' old will that retained his ties to Cindy. He tore the whole lot up, and threw them on the dying flame. The flame went *whoosh*, beyond a cackling. He made sure the will was no longer needed. He too, wanted Cindy to be free of them.

'Thanks Master Barkhor,' a lady grinned at him, who approached the fire to keep warm. The fire suddenly burst loudly on stage, before it quieted down in floating embers, mid-room. The lady jumped out of her skin before Barkhor prevented her falling from fright.

'That was the grandparents' will,' Barkhor explained, 'You've just unburdened me from it. I hope you two enjoy one another for life.'

Now, I felt more challenging. 'Will you marry us?'

Barkhor cried, 'Marry you? I've barely time for myself and four dogs!'

I knew he was horsing around, but then got serious. 'No, really, do you have authority to marry us. I trust you are the leader of sorts in these parts.'

'I don't lead. I just help out,' he answered me. 'You're better off in New Chicago. You should marry there. Anything done out here could be misconstrued, especially since we don't get many like you visiting.'

'Not that they'd want to,' I added. 'Okay.'

'Cindihan O'Myde is yours now, Elias Huer. Do with her as you wish,' Barkhor confirmed.

'You deserve better, in all cases,' I cooed at her, 'I'll help you every step.'

'So devotional you are,' Barkhor said. He kissed her on the forehead and made his way toward helping his community.

And with that, we began our journey back to New Chicago.

CHAPTER XIV

It took some time before I could observe the reaches of New Chicago. I had to get past this deckin' wilderness, however. Cindy and I were tired by now, but we had our supplies. No weaponry. You'd think a fellow like me would have a device or two splintered around the person somewhere. Under the belt. Hidden in a sock, or a musty garment. But no, what I did have was already spent, trying to escape Eri-Cast's kingdom of Arachnia. As I had nothing left, the lone scientist-to-be that I was, I marched on with my young girlfriend.

My relationship with Cindihan was good. Hotting up, even. Without complications. Boring, to say the least, but at least I knew what was best for her. I left her to her own devices; not that she had much, but I allowed her to 'grow up' somewhat before I decided to meddle with her, out of pure enjoyment. I gazed at her plainness in the warm summer sunshine. I thought I had a birthday somewhere, but I lost track of the days. She looked lovely, all warm and fuzzy. Her soul was a delight; I saw her beauty, distraught and clashing with her inner consciousness. Her resourcefulness got us out of many a straggling argument with the hostility of the environment around us.

We walked and wandered about, meandering in our own thoughts. I wanted to meander toward her, but I sensed barriers and thought it best not to. Anarchia was well past us by now; Barkhor, with his bag of favours, a distant memory. I missed him. He was a good chap. He would have been better off with us, constantly rebuilding New Chicago. People like him know the good of society, and those in society.

My twin brother wasn't off-mind either. *Not far off by a long shot.* I thought about him, and wondered how he was faring. I yearned to see him again, even to just touch base with him, just to see that he was alive. It had been so long, yet, it wasn't personal. He was my brother; it was still a wish none-the-less.

And what of Dad? How was he doing, and how would he take the news of me bringing home the young lady, Cindihan? I bet Silage would have a ton to say about it. In fact, I wouldn't be surprised if he were to fight me over her, and force her to choose between us. Now fair is fair, but that would become manic. *She didn't even know the guy!* I was certain his studies on the planet Dracos were just as fruitful as mine were in Anarchia, and further thought again of how he'd get out of the messes I was in during my stay in Arachnia. I guessed I'd have to wait until I reached home to find out.

The one I solely missed out on was Twiki, the quad who knew no bounds. I was sure that Dad put more research into him, maybe changing his programming to become a more *sophisticated* being. I liked him as he was, since I helped in his programming from day to day life, teaching him things. I do hope Dad didn't program the poor fellow out of his endlessly amusing joke-telling. That took some work from me, I'll tell you, and it was a pleasure to witness.

I heard a small voice complaining.

'How much longer is it, Elias? We've been walking for hours!'

Cindihan.

'Time, Cindy, time,' I assured her, 'We'll get there.'

More hours passed. This desert was a foray into forever. A spell was certain, we would be dead within our spiny molecules. The sun by now was at its hottest, and my threadbare outfit yielded all too well to it. However, flickering lights soon flashed up ahead, and I thought we could be saved from the past days of annihilation.

A ship wooshed overhead, above the plain-jane plateau of Anarchia. It was one of those *Ranger-M4* ships. A short, stubby, multi-passenger aircraft that went on exploratory missions beyond our seas. I vaguely remember seeing them fly about in New Chicago, years ago. I just never took notice to them. We stood dumbfounded within our mongrel dignity.

A voice boomed out from the ship. 'Can I give you both a lift?'

Cindy waved frantically at the ship, calling it down to pick us up. 'Yes, please.'

It wasn't like he was doing us any favours!

Still I was amazed at her prowess and forthright approach. Living rough must do that to people, which obviously got the better of her; its knowledge base proving useful to us.

The ship went upon the ground, and out stood a fellow not much taller than me. After a waft of smoke and embers, the pilot crawled out of his ship.

'I'm Lt Clary Busdon. I was on a routine scan of these plains. I thought you both could use transport back to New Chicago.'

Busdon was fair, almost pretty in a masculine sort of way. His flight-suit fitted him like a glove. His grey eyes stood out, above a square jawline.

'You must be Elias Huer, Jr,' he added.

How did he know?

I made my introductions. 'I am, and this is Cindihan O'Myde. Everyone calls her Cindy.'

He cooed at her. 'How do you do, Cindy?'

She giggled, her girlish charm oozed from the rough exterior.

And asked her, 'Would you like to ride my ship?'

She answered quite eagerly, 'Wow, can I?'

'Sure, come on board.' He guided us into the *Ranger*, and started for take-off.

He asked me, 'Where did you find her, or did you both go out this way together?'

'Ah, long story,' I sighed, 'Somewhere on the furtherest reaches of chaos this world had ever known.'

'So, you'd found her among the dead spirits on Anarchia,' he concluded.

This guy was no spoilsport and a genius in his own right! Either that or he was aware of the soddenness of Anarchia.

'It's not that dead out there, Lt. They've got a semi-society, with a live and make-do attitude. I'd picked Cindy up by the rubble. She's quite the resourceful one,' I said.

'Call me Clary. Everyone else does, Elias.'

I blushed at *his* forwardness and looked out the window. The landscape was still barren, but safer within this passing ship. I preferred it that way. I enjoyed looking out, and being with Cindy. At least we were rescued from having to *walk* back to New Chicago.

Things that pass, come and go, *but a passing ship was nothing to sniff about.* It certainly wasn't, when we were out there. Soon, instead of the plain-jane beige topography, I began to see buildings jutting out into the sky and futuristic banter they must be imparting to one another.

I took my boot off to rid myself of the passing menace upon it. A whole load of dust and debris spilled out onto the carpeted floor.

'Uh, please don't do that,' Clary requested, 'I just had this baby cleaned yesterday'.

I put the footwear back on. 'Oh, sorry.' I tried to clean up the crap from my shoe. I did find a waste receptacle and put the gunk into it.

'I like to keep a clean ship. Nothing personal, mind. Tidy comes and tidy goes. You know how it is.'

'Oh, yeah,' I glanced about. This ship, the envy of all other ships, clear around me.

The flight back neared its end, and we docked on the pathways of New Chicago. Someone awaited me, and it wasn't Dad. It wasn't Silage, either. He looked familiar though, someone I saw at the lab or visiting our home, before I left on my *adventure*. It mind-boggled me, but I waited until he introduced himself.

Clary took some bits out with him. 'I hoped you enjoyed your ride back. Good to meet with you Elias and Cindy, and I hope to see you both again soon.'

'You've saved our lives, Clary,' I stated.

'Eh, I'm always saving somebody,' he responded, 'It's the way of things.'

I got off his ship with Cindy and met up with the fellow I saw waiting earlier. He approached us with intent.

'Hello, good to see you again. Won't you come this way,' he said, 'I don't want to discuss personal matters in public.'

Now, if it were an earlier time period, I'd be suspicious. Yet, in our time, Mankind has learned to trust one another. So I had to trust him. I thought I remembered him from long ago. Wait, my mind unscrambled with ease. I remember now, he worked for my father, and helped us at the time of my mother's death. *Pemur Oppenmach.* He designed technological gizbows, do-dads and what-not with Dad. I've seen him at the lab a bunch of times, but now he worked for PMR Industries, trying out the new pyro-magnetic radiation modules.

'Mr Oppenmach,' I extended my hand.

'Master Elias,' he extended his and we shook hands.

'Everybody seems to know me,' I exclaimed.

'Yes, through your father. He was one of the best. An enlightened source of New Chicago. Your absence was most felt by him.'

'Don't I know it,' I sighed, 'But it was he who sent me away.'

'To see if you can look after yourself okay. He wasn't going to keep you tied down to him forever, you know. He did not want that for you.' He went on, looking at Cindy. 'Who's the girl?'

'Cindihan O'Myde. I met her on my outbound travels,' I answered.

'Guess she didn't like the area.'

'No she did not. It was vile, to both of us.'

'I'm sure of it. Anarchia was left undisturbed for some time. Anyone living there, well, they just lived there and minded their own business. I have news for you,' he said morbidly.

Well, what could that be? I couldn't think of what it could be, or what it was in the first place. We just spoke about Dad, and I recalled Dad looked fine. I prayed it would not be about *him*, of all people. He was getting on in years, doddery (like all scientists), but old-age silly, and in good health.

We turned a corner and got into a ship back to our place. The test of time was upon us, as I reached home. I then got the news which would change my life forever.

TO BE CONTINUED.....

www.ingramcontent.com/pod-product-compliance
Lightning Source LLC
LaVergne TN
LVHW091558060526
838200LV00036B/894